j
Carey, M. V.
The three investigators
in The mystery of the
wandering cave man

**DO NOT REMOVE
CARDS FROM POCKET**

3-83

P9-BVC-117

THE MYSTERY OF THE

WANDERING CAVE MAN

The Three Investigators suddenly heard a sound that made their hearts beat faster.

Someone was moving behind the closed door!

Bob made a move toward the door, and Pete caught his arm.

"Don't!" whispered Pete. "Suppose it's . . . *him?*"

He didn't explain. He didn't have to. The other two boys understood.

Suppose the cave man had walked again!

The Three Investigators in

THE MYSTERY OF THE
WANDERING CAVE MAN

by M. V. Carey

Based on characters created by Robert Arthur

Random House New York

Copyright © 1982 by Random House, Inc.
All rights reserved under International and Pan-American Copyright
Conventions. Published in the United States by Random House, Inc.,
New York, and simultaneously in Canada by Random House of
Canada Limited, Toronto.

Library of Congress Cataloging in Publication Data:
Carey, M. V.
   The three investigators in
The mystery of the wandering cave man.
   (Three Investigators mystery series ; no. 34)
   SUMMARY: Three young sleuths investigate the disappearance
of a cave man's bones from a museum and uncover skulduggery
at a science foundation.
   [1. Mystery and detective stories.   2. Museums—Fiction]
I. Arthur, Robert   II. Title.   III. Title: Mystery of the
wandering cave man.   IV. Series.
PZ7.C213Tj   [Fic]   82-3667   AACR2
ISBN: 0-394-85278-8 (pbk.)   ISBN: 0-394-95278-2 (lib. bdg.)

Manufactured in the United States of America
1   2   3   4   5   6   7   8   9   0

Contents

A Word from
Hector Sebastian

Greetings, mystery lovers!

Some of you know the Three Investigators at least as well as I do. I advise you to turn to page three right away and get on with the story. But if you are among those who haven't met the boys as yet, I am delighted to have this chance to introduce them.

Jupiter Jones is the leader of the young detectives, and he enjoys the title of First Investigator. He is a brainy boy and a fanatical reader with an almost photographic memory and an uncanny talent for deduction. Pete

Crenshaw, the Second Investigator, may not be as clever as Jupe, but he's athletic, good-natured, and devoted to his friends. Bob Andrews is in charge of Records and Research. He's a quiet boy, not as athletic as Pete, but still capable of real daring.

In this adventure the Three Investigators leave their home base in Rocky Beach to encounter a man, dead for centuries, who nevertheless walks at night in a remote village. They meet a trio of scientists who pursue strange, and possibly sinister, studies. And the boys find themselves sealed in an ancient crypt when . . .

But I mustn't give away the whole story. If you are curious to know more—and surely you are!—turn to chapter one and begin to read!

HECTOR SEBASTIAN

THE MYSTERY OF THE

WANDERING CAVE MAN

1

The Stranger
in the Fog

"Are you all right?" said a woman's voice.

Jupiter Jones stood still and listened.

The afternoon was thick with fog. Fog muffled the noise of the traffic on the Pacific Coast Highway. It hung like a curtain between The Jones Salvage Yard and the houses across the street. It seemed to press in on Jupe. He felt cold and lonely, as if he were the only person in all the world.

But someone had spoken, and now there were footsteps. Outside, just beyond the gates of the salvage yard, someone was walking.

Then a man spoke, and two people appeared, moving like shadows in the gray light. The man was bent over, and as he walked his feet made slow, scuffling noises on the pavement. The woman was girlish and thin, with long, fair hair that hung straight about her face.

"Here's a bench," she said, and she guided the man to a seat near the office. "You rest a minute. You should have let me drive. It was too much for you."

"Can I help?" Jupe moved closer to the pair.

The man put a hand to his head and looked around in a dazed fashion. "We're looking for . . . for . . ."

He caught at the young woman's hand. "You do it," he said. "Find out where we . . . where we . . ."

"Harborview Lane," said the young woman to Jupe. "We have to go to Harborview Lane."

"It's down the highway and off Sunset," said Jupe. "Look, if your friend is ill, I can call a doctor and—"

"No!" cried the man. "Not now! We're late!"

Jupe bent toward the man. He saw a face that was gray and glistening with sweat.

"Tired!" said the man. "So tired!"

He pressed his hands to his forehead. "Such a headache!" There was surprise and dismay in his voice. "So strange! I never have headaches!"

"Please let me call a doctor!" begged Jupe.

The stranger pulled himself up. "Be all right in a minute, but now I can't . . . can't . . ."

He sank back against the side of the office, and his breathing became heavy and harsh. Then his face crumpled and twisted. "Hurts!" he said.

Jupe took hold of the man's hand. The flesh was cold and clammy to his touch. The man gazed at Jupe. His eyes were fixed and did not blink.

Suddenly it was very quiet in the salvage yard.

The young woman bent to touch the man. She made a sound like a whimper of pain.

There were brisk footsteps on the pavement, and Jupiter's aunt Mathilda came through the gate. She saw the man on the bench and the girl bending over him. She saw Jupe kneeling in front of him.

"Jupiter, what is it?" said Aunt Mathilda. "Is something wrong? Shall I call the paramedics?"

"Yes," said Jupe. "You . . . you call them. But I don't think it will do any good. I think he's dead!"

Afterward Jupe was to remember a confusion of lights and sirens and men hurrying in the fog. The blonde girl wept in Aunt Mathilda's arms.

People clustered at the gate of the salvage yard, and there was a terrible hush when the stretcher was put in the ambulance. Then there were more sirens, and Jupe and Aunt Mathilda were driving to the hospital with the blonde girl between them in the car.

Jupiter felt that he moved through a dream, gray and unreal.

But the hospital was grim reality. There was a corridor where people hurried about. There was a waiting room stale with cigarette smoke. Jupe, Aunt Mathilda, and the blonde girl sat and leafed through old magazines. After a long, long while a doctor came.

"I'm sorry," said the doctor to the girl. "We couldn't do anything. It's . . . sometimes it's best that way. You aren't a relative, are you?"

She shook her head.

"There will be an autopsy," he said. "I'm sorry. It's usual in cases where someone dies without a doctor. It was probably a cerebral accident—a ruptured blood vessel in the head. The autopsy will confirm it. Do you know how we can get in touch with his family?"

She shook her head again. "No. I'll have to call the foundation."

She began to sob, and a nurse came and led her away. Jupiter and Aunt Mathilda waited. After a long while the girl came back. She had

made a telephone call from the nursing direc-
tor's office.

"They'll come from the foundation," she told
Jupiter and Aunt Mathilda.

Jupiter wondered what the foundation might
be, but he didn't ask. Aunt Mathilda announced
that they must all have a good strong cup of tea.
She took the girl by the arm and propelled her
out of the waiting room and down a corridor to
the hospital coffee shop.

For a while they sat without talking and drank
their tea, but finally the girl spoke.

"He was very nice," she said. She went on in
a low voice, staring down at her rough hands
with their jagged, bitten nails. The dead man
was Dr. Karl Birkensteen, a famous geneticist.
He had been working at the Spicer Foundation,
studying various animals for the effects his
experiments had on their intelligence—and
that of their offspring. The girl worked there,
too, helping to care for the animals.

"I've heard of the Spicer Foundation," said
Jupe. "It's down the coast, isn't it? Near San
Diego?"

She nodded. "It's in a little town in the hills
there, on the road that goes over to the desert."

"The town is called Citrus Grove," said Jupe.

For the first time the girl smiled. "Yes. That's
nice. I mean, not many people know about

Citrus Grove. Even if they've heard of the foundation, they don't know the name of the town."

"Jupiter reads a great deal," said Aunt Mathilda, "and he remembers most of what he reads. However, I don't know about the town, or the foundation either. What is it?"

"It's an institution that fosters independent scientific research," said Jupiter. Suddenly he sounded like a college professor discoursing on some little-known subject. It was a way he had when he explained subjects in which he was well versed. Aunt Mathilda was accustomed to it, and she did not seem to notice, but the blonde girl stared at him curiously.

"Abraham Spicer was a manufacturer of plastics," said Jupe. "His company produced such items as dish drainers and food containers. He made millions in his lifetime. However, he never achieved his real ambition, which was to be a physicist. He therefore instructed that when he died, his money was to go into a trust fund. The income from the fund was to support a foundation where scientists could do original, and perhaps revolutionary, research in their special fields."

"Do you always talk like that?" asked the girl.

Aunt Mathilda smiled. "Too frequently he

does. It may have something to do with all that reading."

"Oh," said the girl. "Okay. I mean, that's nice, I guess. I didn't tell you my name, did I? It's Hess. Eleanor Hess. Not that it matters."

"Of course it matters," said Aunt Mathilda.

"Well, what I mean is, it's not as if I were really anybody. I'm not famous or anything."

"Which is not to say that you're nobody," said Aunt Mathilda firmly. "I'm pleased to meet you, Eleanor Hess. I am Mrs. Titus Jones, and this is my nephew, Jupiter Jones."

Eleanor Hess smiled. Then she looked away quickly, as if she were afraid of revealing too much of herself.

"Tell us more about your work at this Spicer Foundation," said Aunt Mathilda. "You said you take care of the animals. What kind of animals?"

"They're experimental animals," said Eleanor. "White rats and chimpanzees and a horse."

"A horse?" echoed Aunt Mathilda. "They keep a horse in a laboratory?"

"Oh, no. Blaze lives in the stable. But she's an experimental animal just the same. Dr. Birkensteen used isotopes or something on her mother. Her *dam* is what you'd say, I guess. Anyway, that did something to her chromosomes. I don't understand it, but she's really smart for a horse. She does arithmetic."

Aunt Mathilda and Jupe both stared.

"Oh, nothing complicated," said Eleanor hastily. "If you put two apples in front of her, and then three apples, she knows it's five apples. She stamps five times. I . . . I suppose that isn't really so great, but horses don't come awfully smart. Their heads are the wrong shape. Dr. Birkensteen's chimps are the clever ones. They talk in sign language. They can say some complicated things."

"I see," said Aunt Mathilda. "And what did Dr. Birkensteen plan to do with these animals, once he had them properly educated?"

"I don't think he was going to do anything with them," she said softly. "Not really. He didn't care about smart horses and talking chimps. He wanted to help people be better. You have to start with animals, don't you? It wouldn't be right to start with a human baby, would it?"

Aunt Mathilda shuddered.

Eleanor looked away, retreating into a cocoon of shyness. "You really don't have to stay with me," she said. "You've been great, but I'm okay now. Dr. Terreano and Mrs. Collinwood will be here soon, and they'll talk to the doctor and . . . and . . ."

She bowed her head and the tears started again.

"There, now," said Aunt Mathilda quietly. "Of course we'll stay."

And stay they did until a tall, bony, gray-haired man came into the coffee shop. Eleanor introduced him as Dr. Terreano. He had with him a plump, sixtyish woman who wore enormous false eyelashes and a curly, flaming red wig. She was Mrs. Collinwood, and she took Eleanor out to the car while Dr. Terreano went to find the doctor who had attended Dr. Birkensteen.

Aunt Mathilda shook her head when she and Jupe were alone. "Strange people!" she said. "Imagine doing things to an animal so that its offspring will be changed. That Terreano person who came in just now—what do you suppose he does?"

"Some sort of research, if he's at the Spicer Foundation," said Jupe.

Aunt Mathilda frowned. "Strange people," she said again. "And that foundation—I would not like to go there. Once those scientists start poking and prying and changing things around, there's no telling where they'll stop. It's not natural! Terrible things could happen!"

Bad Blood!

Aunt Mathilda told Uncle Titus that night about the scientist who had come through the fog and died in their salvage yard. She said very little about the Spicer Foundation, however, and when Jupiter mentioned the place, she quickly changed the subject. The idea of genetic experiments plainly upset and frightened her. But she did not have a chance to forget the Spicer Foundation entirely, for as the cool, gray days of spring passed, that institution for scientific research was in the news again and again.

First there were the reports on Dr. Birkensteen's death. As the physician at the hospital had suspected, Birkensteen had suffered a stroke. There were brief accounts of his work in genetics, and the reports concluded with the information that the body was to be shipped to the East for burial.

Scarcely a week later the Spicer Foundation was involved in an astounding discovery, and newspaper people swarmed into the little town of Citrus Grove to cover the story. An archaeologist named James Brandon, a scientist in residence at the foundation, had discovered the bones of a prehistoric creature in a cave on the outskirts of the town.

"What a great mystery!" exclaimed Jupe. It was an afternoon in May, and Jupe and his friends were in the old mobile home trailer that was Headquarters for the detective firm they had started some time before. Jupe had the newspaper spread out on the desk. Bob Andrews was reorganizing the files while Pete Crenshaw was cleaning the equipment in the tiny crime lab the boys had set up.

Pete looked around. "What's a mystery?" he asked.

"The cave man of Citrus Grove," said Jupe. "Is it really human? How old is it? James Brandon, the archaeologist who found it, calls it a hominid. That could mean a man, or it could mean a manlike animal. Is it prehuman, or something else?"

"Brandon is going to be on television this afternoon," said Bob. "My folks were talking about it at breakfast. He'll be a guest on the *Bob Engel Show* at five o'clock."

Pete wiped off the counter in the lab. "You want to watch?" he said.

"You bet I do," said Jupiter Jones.

There was a small black-and-white television set on the bookcase near Jupe's desk. Uncle Titus had acquired it on one of his buying trips. It had been out of commission when it came into the salvage yard. But Jupe had a knack for fixing things, and he had put the set in working order and had installed it in Headquarters. Now it flickered to life, and the boys saw Bob Engel, the talk show host, smiling at the television audience.

"Our first guest today is Dr. James Brandon," said Engel. "He's the man who discovered the fossil remains of a prehistoric man in a cave right here in southern California."

The camera pulled back, and the boys saw a lean, rugged-looking man with close-cut fair hair. Next to him was a shorter, rather paunchy man wearing a cowboy shirt, a wide belt with an ornate buckle, and high-heeled boots.

"Today Dr. Brandon is accompanied by Mr.

Newt McAfee. Mr. McAfee is a merchant in the town of Citrus Grove, and he owns the land where the cave man was discovered."

"Right!" said the chubby man. "And that's McAfee: Mack—like in Mack truck—A-fee. A fee's the money the dentist charges you to yank a tooth. Don't forget it, 'cause you're going to be hearing that name lots from now on."

Bob Engel forced a smile, then turned his attention to his other guest.

"All right, now, Dr. Brandon," he said. "Could you give us a little background, in case some of us haven't read about the discovery of the fossils?"

The fair-haired man straightened in his chair. "It was pure luck that I found them," he said. "I went out for a walk a week or so ago, just after the rains stopped, and I noticed that there had been a small landslide on the hill above Newt McAfee's meadow. Part of the slope had come down, and there was an opening in the side of the hill. When I got closer, I saw that there was a cave, and I could see the skull inside. It was nearly buried in the mud on the floor of the cave, and I didn't know what I had at first, so—"

"You don't have nothing, buddy," interrupted the man next to Brandon. "I'm the one that's got it!"

Brandon ignored this. "I went back to the Spicer house to get a flashlight," he said.

"And when he got back to my field, I was waiting with a shotgun," said McAfee. "Come trespassing on my property and I'll take notice!"

Brandon took a deep breath. He seemed to be controlling his temper with difficulty. "I explained what I'd seen," he said. "We looked closer, and I knew for sure that it was a skull!"

"An old one!" cried McAfee. "Been there for thousands of years."

"In addition to the skull," said Brandon, "most of the skeleton remains. I haven't been able to really study it yet, but there are similarities to very old fossils discovered in Africa."

"And is it a man?" asked Engel.

Brandon frowned. "Who's to say exactly what makes a being a man—a human? There are definite hominid characteristics, but it isn't what we would recognize as a modern man. I'm almost sure that it is older than any hominids found in America so far."

Brandon leaned forward. His tone now was enthusiastic. "There is a theory that the American Indian descended from Mongolian hunters who migrated from Siberia to Alaska during the last ice age. That was about eight thousand years ago, at a time when so much ocean water was frozen into ice that the level of the sea was quite low. The ocean bottom in the narrows between Siberia and Alaska was exposed, so Asian tribesmen could simply walk across from one continent to the other, following the game they hunted to the New World. The theory has it that they then spread out and settled in various places, and some of them kept going until they reached the tip of South America.

"That's the accepted theory. It's the one you'll find in most schoolbooks. But now and then someone pops up with a different explanation. Some of these mavericks say that man lived on this continent long before the time the nomads are supposed to have crossed that land bridge. Some even claim that modern man really originated in America, and that he migrated the other way, to Asia and Europe."

"And do the fossils in the cave at Citrus Grove support this theory?" asked Engel.

"I can't say right now," said Brandon. "At this point I can't even be sure how old those bones are. But we have much of the skeleton, and—"

"You mean *I* have the skeleton," said Newt McAfee. He glowed with perspiration and delight. "And that little guy in my cave sure is a human, right enough. Ain't anything else it could be, is there? So if he's been there two or three million years—"

"Now wait a minute!" cried Brandon.

"You said yourself you didn't know how old he was!" insisted McAfee. "Had to be much older than eight or ten thousand was what you said. You was sure enough of that when you first saw him. So that means humans did start up here in America, and that little guy in my cave could be the great-granddaddy of us all. Maybe it was his kids and grandkids that went across them straits to Asia and started humanity on its way. Maybe the Garden of Eden wasn't someplace over there, like we always thought. Supposing it was in Bakersfield or Fresno. Wouldn't that be a lick?"

"You're jumping to conclusions," said Brandon in a dogged way. "When we have a chance to properly study the find—"

"Ain't going to be no studying done!" declared McAfee.

Brandon spun around and glared at McAfee.

"That little guy's been in my cave right along, and he's going to stay there!" said McAfee. "Ain't nobody going to haul him away and cut him up and look at him through a microscope. And if you think the lines of people waiting to get into Marineland and Magic Mountain are long, just wait'll you see the lines of people who'll want to see a real cave man!"

"You're going to put the fossils on display?" cried Brandon. "But you can't! We aren't sure how old the bones are, or . . ."

"The bones are old enough," McAfee announced. "What we've got right here is the beginnings of civilization, and everybody's interested in that!"

"You ignorant lout!" shouted Brandon. "You haven't any idea what you're talking about!"

"I'm talking about what may be the first man." McAfee looked full at the camera. "That's why I come on this show. I want everybody to know that I'm getting my place ready, and as soon as I can, I'll open my cave for visitors. It'll be like those other wonderful places in California, and—"

"You imbecile!" shouted Brandon. He lurched out of his chair.

The camera quickly moved in close so that only Bob Engel could be seen. There was some shouting off camera, and a scuffling noise. Then Bob Engel said hastily, "That's all for this exciting portion of our show. We're out of time, thank heavens. Now stay tuned for an important message from Nodust furniture polish, and then we'll be back with . . ."

Pete turned off the television. "Wow!" he said. "Things really got out of hand there. Brandon looked like he was going to pound that McAfee guy right into the ground."

"I didn't like McAfee much myself," said

Jupe, "and if he won't let Brandon remove the bones . . ."

"Can he stop Brandon?" said Bob.

"I should think so, if the cave is on his property. What a maddening situation for an archaeologist to be in—to find something so exciting and then not be able to evaluate it! And probably there's been bad blood between those two men from the beginning, if McAfee ran for his gun when he saw Brandon at the cave. A bad situation! And Brandon's got a temper. It's the sort of thing that could end in . . . in . . ."

"Bloodshed?" said Pete.

"Yes. Yes, that's just how it could end—in bloodshed!"

An Unusual Welcome

After that first explosive interview, James Brandon did not appear on television again. It was Newt McAfee who was seen on several of the talk shows, and as spring turned to summer, the chubby merchant from Citrus Grove gave interviews to any reporter who would stand still and listen. By the middle of July most people in southern California knew about his cave and his cave man. Then the paid advertisements began to appear. The cave would be opened to the public early in August.

During the last week of July, Jupiter had a

timely encounter with his neighbor Les Wolf.

Wolf was a contractor who installed ovens and stoves and dishwashers in restaurants and hotels. He lived in a big frame house down the street from The Jones Salvage Yard. On that July day Jupe was riding his bike past the Wolf home when he saw Mr. Wolf trying to coax a kitten out from under a hedge. Jupe stopped to lend a hand. He approached the hedge from one side and stamped his foot, and the little cat scooted out the other side and into Mr. Wolf's grip.

"There, now," said Wolf. He grinned at Jupe. "Thanks, Jupe. My wife would never have forgiven me if the cat had gotten away and been run over or something."

Wolf started for the house with the kitten cradled in his arms. But then he stopped and turned back toward Jupiter. "Say, you know that little town down the coast? The place where they found the cave man? I'm putting in a new kitchen in a restaurant there later this week. Didn't your aunt tell my wife that you've been following that cave man story in the newspapers?"

"You bet I have!" said Jupe eagerly. "The cave man goes on view this Saturday. Are you taking the big truck to Citrus Grove? You wouldn't need a helper on that job, would you?"

"You're too young, and besides, you're not in the union," said Mr. Wolf. "Hal Knight is going along to help. But if you don't mind riding in the back of the truck, along with my gear . . ."

"You bet I don't!" said Jupe quickly. "Could my friends Bob and Pete come too?"

"Sure. Only you boys will have to find a place to stay. It'll take me about three days to finish the job, and the couple who own the restaurant will put me up. They've got room for Hal, too, but they don't have room for any more."

"That'll be all right," said Jupe. "We can bring our sleeping bags and camp out."

Jupe hurried home to call his friends and to get permission from Aunt Mathilda and Uncle Titus to make the trip. On Friday morning, when Les Wolf's truck rolled out of Rocky Beach, Jupe, Pete, and Bob were aboard.

Mr. Wolf drove south for nearly two hours, then turned off the main highway and headed east, up into the hills. The road turned and dipped and climbed. The boys saw orange groves on either side, open fields, stands of trees, and broad meadows where cattle grazed.

After half an hour the truck slowed to go through a town called Centerdale, beyond which were more miles of trees and groves and grassland. Then at last a sign informed them: "Entering Citrus Grove. Speed laws strictly enforced."

Citrus Grove was hardly more than a hamlet. The boys saw a supermarket, two gas stations, a car dealership, and a tiny motel called The Elms. They passed the town swimming pool and then an abandoned railroad station that looked bleak and dusty. In the center of the village a little park lined one side of the street and a row of narrow stores lined the other. The boys saw a bank, a hardware store, a drugstore, and the public library. But though the town was small, there were crowds everywhere. A neon "No Vacancy" sign flashed at the motel, and outside the Lazy Daze Café a long line of people was waiting to be seated.

"All that publicity about the cave man," said Bob. "It's really drawing the crowds."

Jupe grinned at the sight of a crowded hamburger stand that advertised dinosaur burgers. "That's getting into the swing of things," he said.

Les Wolf turned onto a side road beyond the park and pulled to the curb. He leaned out to call to the boys.

"The Happy Hunter Restaurant is down this way half a mile or so," he said. "I called the owner last night and he said the campground near town is full. He says you're to see Newt McAfee in that gray frame house at the head of Main Street. McAfee's finding places for people to stay."

"Not that guy from TV!" exclaimed Pete.

"I'm afraid so," said Jupe.

The boys scrambled out of the truck.

"Check with me at the Happy Hunter on Monday," Wolf told them. Then he drove away.

Newt McAfee's house looked pleasant enough when the boys started toward it. In front it had a wide porch and a small lawn. As the boys neared the place, however, they saw that the house badly needed paint and the curtains at the windows were gray and limp. Some of the shutters were missing slats. The lawn was mostly crabgrass.

"Looks seedy, doesn't it?" said Bob. "I thought McAfee owned the hardware store and the car dealership."

"Maybe that doesn't make him prosperous in a town this size," said Jupe.

A sign was tacked to the porch railing of the McAfee house. It advised visitors who needed accommodations to go around to the back. The boys trudged obediently around the house, and they saw a meadow that stretched away from the road to a patch of woodland. Quite close to the house was a barn, silvery with age. On the side of the house that was farthest from town, the meadow extended a short way along the road until it ran into a nearby hill. Huddled against the hillside was a spanking new building. It was trim and modern, built of redwood, and windowless. Above the double doors a sign read: "Entrance to Cave Man Cavern."

"Hey, hey!" said Pete. "The guy is making a real production out of it."

"Do you want something?" said a soft voice behind the boys.

They turned, and Jupe saw pale hair and a pale face. He remembered a bleak and foggy day in Rocky Beach, and a man who walked in from the highway to die.

"Oh!" said Eleanor Hess. "It's you!"

"Hi." Jupe put his hand out and she took it.

"I . . . uh . . . I was going to write to your aunt," she said. "You were so nice. But I thought maybe you wouldn't want to be bothered."

"I'm glad we could help," said Jupe, and he introduced Bob and Pete.

As Eleanor acknowledged the introductions, the back door of the house opened and a plump woman with short, frizzy hair looked out.

"Ellie, what do those boys want?" she called.

She spoke rudely, as if the boys couldn't hear her.

"Aunt Thalia, this is Jupiter Jones," said Eleanor. She looked flushed and unhappy. "I told you about him. He and his aunt helped me when Dr. Birkensteen was sick up in Rocky Beach. And this is Pete Crenshaw and this is Bob Andrews. They're Jupiter's friends. I guess they've come to see the cave man. Aunt Thalia, couldn't we put them up?"

The man who had been on so many talk shows appeared suddenly in the doorway beside the woman. Eleanor Hess introduced the boys again, and Jupe's jaw dropped when he realized that Aunt Thalia must be Newt McAfee's wife—which meant that Newt was Eleanor's uncle!

"So you're the one who was so nice to Ellie," said Newt. "Well, we'd be glad to put you up. We don't have room in the house for the three of you, but you can spread your bedrolls in the loft above the barn and use the old outhouse behind the barn. There's a faucet on the side of the house for washing."

McAfee's small eyes crinkled. "I'll make you a real good rate. Just ten dollars a night for the three of you."

"Uncle Newt!" cried Eleanor Hess.

"Now, there, missy!" said McAfee. He shot a

warning look at Eleanor, and she looked away.

"You can't get in anyplace for ten dollars," McAfee told the boys.

"Why don't we just find a clearing in the woods?" said Bob. He gestured toward the trees beyond the meadow.

"Fire danger's high this year," said McAfee. "Them woods are closed to campers."

Jupe took out his wallet and held a ten-dollar bill toward McAfee. "Here," he said. "This is for tonight."

"Good enough." McAfee pocketed the money. "Ellie, show the boys where the outside faucet is."

"Now, you boys be careful," warned Thalia McAfee. "Don't you mess things up or set fire to anything."

"You don't smoke, do you?" asked McAfee.

"We don't smoke," said Pete sullenly. "Hey, Jupe, we shouldn't bother the McAfees. Why don't we go down to the little park in town and . . ."

"No camping in the park," said McAfee. "Besides, there's an automatic sprinkler system there that goes off at midnight every night."

McAfee went chuckling into the house, and Eleanor started toward the barn, her face red with shame.

"I'm sorry," she said. "Listen, if you stay over

tomorrow, don't pay him. I've got some money and I'll take care of it."

"It's okay," said Jupe. "Don't worry about it."

"I hate it when he does things like that," said Eleanor bitterly. "And I'm never supposed to say anything because . . . well, because he and Aunt Thalia have taken care of me since I was eight. My parents died in a car accident."

Each of the boys wondered privately how well McAfee and his wife took care of Eleanor. She was very thin, and she had a faded, worn look.

"Aunt Thalia and my mom were sisters," she went on. "I'd have had to go to an orphanage if Aunt Thalia hadn't taken me in."

She opened the door and the boys followed her into the dusty dimness of the barn. They saw a shining new pickup truck there, and a big four-door sedan that bristled with chrome. They also saw the heaped-up debris of years —bundles of yellowed newspapers and piles of old cartons and a jumble of tools rusting on a workbench.

A ladder on the back wall led to the loft, and the boys climbed to a shadowed, suffocating area under the roof. There was a window thick with dirt and cobwebs. When Jupe opened it, coolness and fresh air swept in.

"You want me to get you some towels?"

Eleanor called from below.

"That's okay," Pete called back. "We brought our own stuff."

Still she lingered at the bottom of the ladder. At last she called, "I'm going up to the foundation pretty soon. Would you like to come see the animals?"

It was plainly the nicest thing she could offer. Jupe leaned over the edge of the loft. "Do you know the archaeologist who found the bones?" he asked.

"Dr. Brandon? Sure. You want to meet him? I can introduce you if he's home."

"I've been wanting to meet him ever since I heard about the fossils," said Jupe. "Has he formed any theories about the age of the bones? Does he know how they got into the cave?"

Eleanor grimaced. "Everybody's so excited about that cave man. But he's so ugly. He must have looked like a gorilla, only much, much smaller."

Suddenly she looked alarmed. "Don't you go near that cave when there's nobody here," she warned. "Uncle Newt's keeping a loaded shotgun behind the kitchen door. He says people will pay plenty to see the cave man, and if anybody tries to interfere, he'll blow him full of holes!"

"He wouldn't be talking about the archaeologist, would he?" questioned Jupe.

"Yes. Or anybody who tried to tamper with the cave man. I'm scared that something's going to happen—something really bad!"

Eleanor Tells a Lie

The Spicer Foundation was a sprawling house on a hill a half mile up the road past McAfee's place. It had no fence to protect its smooth green lawns, but there were stone gateposts and a gate. The boys followed Eleanor up the drive to the house. She opened the door and went in without knocking.

There was no entry hall. Eleanor and the boys were immediately in a big living room. James Brandon was there too. He was pacing, and he paused to scowl when Eleanor introduced the boys.

"You came for the three-ring circus," he said. It sounded like an accusation.

"To see the cave man?" said Pete. "Yes, we did."

"You and four million other people," said Brandon. He started to pace again. "They're going to trample everything. If there are more fossils in these hills, they'll be destroyed. If I had a gun . . ."

"You'd shoot them all," said a calm voice.

The boys turned. A tall, mournful-looking man had walked into the room. Jupiter recognized him immediately as the man who had come to the Rocky Beach hospital the night Karl Birkensteen died. On that occasion he had worn a threadbare gray suit. Now he was dressed in faded khaki shorts and a polo shirt. He sat down in an armchair near the fireplace and stared at his own bony knees.

"Dr. Terreano, you've met Jupiter Jones," said Eleanor Hess.

Terreano looked surprised. "I have?"

"He helped me when I was in Rocky Beach with Dr. Birkensteen," Eleanor explained. "He was at the hospital, remember?"

"Oh, yes. I recall now. Nice to see you again—and under happier circumstances."

Terreano smiled and suddenly appeared much younger.

"Dr. Terreano is an archaeologist too," said Eleanor. "He's writing a book."

Terreano grinned. "We are always writing books."

"Oh, yes!" said Jupe suddenly. "I know! You wrote *Ancient Enemy!*"

Terreano's eyebrows shot up. "You read that?"

"Yes," said Jupe. "I found the book at the library. It's fascinating, but discouraging. If man has always had a need to battle his fellow man, and if he always will . . ."

"Sad, isn't it?" said Terreano. "Our violence is inborn. It's one of our distinguishing characteristics, along with a large brain and the ability to walk upright."

"Oh, rot!" exclaimed Brandon. "Man is not inherently violent. You've misinterpreted the evidence."

"Have I?" Terreano looked around him. "Consider, if you will, Abraham Spicer," he said. "Spicer believed in helping humanity. He set up this foundation, and wasn't that noble! But Spicer was also a killer. He was a big-game hunter."

Torreano gestured toward the mantel. The head of some delicate horned creature was there, its dead eyes staring toward the windows. On the wall above some bookcases there were other animal heads—a tiger, a puma, and a massive water buffalo. The pelts of bears and lions and leopards were strewn over the floor.

"If you kill a wild animal instead of another man," said Terreano, "you are allowed to bring the carcass home and stuff it. There was a time when it was equally acceptable to crush the bones of an enemy and eat the marrow."

"You are absolutely wrong!" shouted Brandon.

"You get so angry whenever we have this discussion," said Terreano. "It almost proves my point."

A short, bald man came bustling in just then. "Are you discussing bone marrow again?" he said. "I hate to hear about bone marrow before I've had my lunch."

Eleanor introduced Dr. Elwood Hoffer. "Dr. Hoffer is an immunologist," she told the boys. "He has a lot of white rats that are really kind of sweet. Could I show the rats to Jupiter and his friends?"

"You can, provided they don't touch anything in the lab," said Hoffer.

"Of course they won't," said Eleanor.

The boys followed her out to a long hall that ran at a right angle to the front of the house.

"The workrooms and laboratories open off this hall," Eleanor explained. "Dr. Hoffer's lab is here."

She ushered them to the next door, and they found themselves in a small washroom. Eleanor produced four surgical masks. "Here," she said. "Put these on." She fixed hers in place, then drew on a pair of heavy rubber gloves.

She opened another door into a huge room bright with sunlight. Against the walls were dozens of cages enclosed in glass, and small creatures darted and scuttled in each cage.

"Don't go too close and don't touch anything," warned Eleanor. She began to feed the rats, moving quietly from cage to cage.

"These rats are very special," she said. "Dr. Hoffer took away some of their immunities, so you have to watch that they don't catch cold or anything. That's the reason for our masks. Some of them have no way to fight off infections."

"That doesn't seem very helpful," said Bob. "If they can't fight off infections, won't they die?"

"I suppose some of them will eventually," said Eleanor. "But Dr. Hoffer believes that we get some diseases just *because* we're immune! Our bodies manufacture special cells that eat up viruses and bacteria, but sometimes those same cells can hurt us. Maybe we get arthritis from our immune reactions, or stomach ulcers, or even some kinds of insanity."

"Wow!" said Pete. He sounded frightened.

"But without immunities we'd get smallpox," said Bob, "and . . . and measles, and . . ."

"I know," said Eleanor. "What Dr. Hoffer is trying to do is find ways to control immunities so that we're protected, but we aren't hurt."

"Wonderful!" said Jupiter. "And Dr. Terreano is writing a new book."

"Dr. Brandon is writing a book too," said Eleanor. "His is about the person in the locked cabinet in his room."

"A person?" said Bob. "Locked in a cabinet?"

"It's a fossil person," said Eleanor. "He found the bones in Africa and put them together like a jigsaw puzzle to make a whole skeleton. He measures the bones and takes pictures of them and looks things up in his books."

"He wants to work with the fossils in the cave the same way, doesn't he?" said Jupiter.

"Yes." Eleanor looked unhappy. "My uncle won't let him."

Eleanor had finished feeding the rats. She and the boys returned to the washroom, where she took off her mask and gloves and dropped them into a covered container near the sink. The boys dropped their masks in, too, and they all went back into the hall.

"Now you'll see the chimps!" she said.

The laboratory that had been used by Dr. Birkensteen was at the end of the corridor. It was bigger than Hoffer's lab. The two chimpanzees that lived in it shared a cage near the window. There were toys and balls in the cage, and a little blackboard where the chimps could scribble with colored chalk.

The animals shrieked with excitement when they saw Eleanor, and the bigger one held out his arms.

"Hi, there!" she said. She opened the door of the cage, and the big chimp came out and took her hand.

"You happy?" she asked. "Did you sleep well last night?"

The chimp closed his eyes briefly and let his head drop to one side. Then he pointed to the clock on the wall and drew circles in the air with one finger.

"You slept long?" asked Eleanor.

The chimp jumped up and down and clapped.

The second chimp got out of the cage and climbed up on one of the laboratory tables.

"Careful!" warned Eleanor.

The animal looked with longing at a shelf lined with jars of chemicals.

"No, no! Don't touch!" said Eleanor. She turned to the boys and laughed. "The chimps remind me so much of toddlers. They want to grab everything within reach and play with it."

Turning away from the shelf, the chimp took an empty beaker from the table, climbed down to the floor, and began to roll the beaker across the room like a toy. Eleanor took fruit and milk from a refrigerator and cereal and bowls from a cupboard.

"They do understand, don't they?" said Jupe as she poured cereal into the bowls.

"Yes. And they can use signs to say some complicated things. Dr. Birkensteen claimed they communicate as well as most kindergarten children. I don't know real sign language, so I can't judge, but I think they're funny and cute, and they sure let me know what they want."

"What will happen to them now?" asked Bob.

Eleanor sighed. "I don't know. The members of the board of the foundation are going to meet next month. They'll probably decide what to do with the animals. The foundation bought them for Dr. Birkensteen—those and a lot more. Most of them died."

Eleanor put bowls of cereal and plates of fruit on a little table, and the chimps scrambled into small chairs and ate. When they finished,

Eleanor coaxed them back to their cage. They both screamed in protest and tried to cling to her.

"It's okay," she said soothingly. "I'll be back soon. Don't get so upset."

The boys watched, and Jupe felt that for the first time he was seeing Eleanor behave as if she were sure of what she was doing. Certainly she looked happier than she had at the McAfees' shabby house.

"They miss Dr. Birkensteen," she said now. "I miss him too. He was nice, even when he wasn't feeling well."

"Had he been ill?" asked Jupe. "Somehow I had the idea that his attack in Rocky Beach was sudden."

"It was," said Eleanor, "but he'd been different for a while before that. He'd fall asleep sitting in his chair. Sometimes he'd doze off while the chimps were out of the cage, and they'd run all over and wreck the place. I went with him the day he . . . he died because it didn't seem as if he should go all that way by himself."

"Why did he go to Rocky Beach that day?" Jupe asked.

The question was an idle one. Jupe asked it only to make conversation. But suddenly Eleanor flushed.

"He was . . . was . . . I don't know really."
She looked away and abruptly went to the door.

Pete and Jupe exchanged glances as she left
the room.

"Now what's the matter?" said Pete softly.
"Did you say something wrong?"

Jupe frowned. "She's lying. You can tell she's
lying. But why should she lie? What could she
be covering up?"

A Visit with
a Dead Man

The scientists were gone when Eleanor and the boys returned to the living room. A plump woman was there straightening the sofa cushions, and a dark-haired young man was washing the small-paned glass doors that led out to the terrace and the swimming pool.

"Morning, Eleanor," said the woman. "I see you've brought some friends with you. That's nice."

Jupe recognized the woman as soon as she spoke. It was Mrs. Collinwood, who had come to help Eleanor the day Dr. Birkensteen died.

She now had on an ash-blond wig instead of a red one, but her eyelashes were as thick and dark as ever. She fluttered them coyly as Eleanor introduced the boys.

"Ah, yes!" she said as she shook hands with Jupe. "I remember. You're the nice young man who was so good to Eleanor. You know, I thought at the time you're so like my dear Charles. Charles Collinwood, that is. My last husband, and really my favorite. Such a kind man, although a bit inclined to be chubby."

Mrs. Collinwood was a talker, and the boys realized quickly that she was off and running. There was little they could do except be still and let the torrent of words wash over them.

Mrs. Collinwood happily told them about her first husband, who had sold insurance, and her second husband, who had been a film editor, and about Charles, her favorite husband, who had been a veterinarian.

"Not that they weren't *all* dear men," said Mrs. Collinwood. "They all died young. So sad. Then I came to live here as housekeeper for the foundation. The scientists were frightening at first. So stern, and always thinking. But once you get to know them, not so different from other men. Dear Dr. Terreano always talks about how violent humans are, but he's so kind he wouldn't swat a fly. And Dr. Brandon insists we aren't violent, and yet he has such a temper. He shouldn't spend so much time with your Uncle Newt, Eleanor. It only upsets him."

"I know," said Eleanor meekly.

Mrs. Collinwood trotted away then, and the young man who was washing the windows dropped his brush into his bucket of water. "You giving your friends the ten-dollar tour?" he asked Eleanor.

She looked annoyed, but she introduced him. "This is Frank," she said. "Frank DiStefano. He helps out here at the foundation, like I do."

The young man grinned. "Hi. Glad to meet you. Ellie, I'm sorry about last night. I got a flat tire and it held me up until . . . well, it was so late I figured you wouldn't still be waiting."

"It's not important," said Eleanor, and she led the boys out through the library, which was next to the living room, and then through a little square entryway on the far side of the house.

The stable was about fifty yards from the house. Eleanor marched to it without speaking. Once she was with Blaze, the horse that had been Dr. Birkensteen's special charge, her mood changed, and again she seemed happier. She groomed the horse and talked to it and petted it, and she proudly showed the boys how it could add. She put four apples on the partition around its stall.

"How many?" she said.

The horse stamped four times.

"There you go!" Eleanor applauded and then fed the apples to the horse.

The boys left Eleanor in the stable and went back down the hill and into town for lunch. The streets were more crowded than ever. The boys decided to pass up the dinosaur burger stand, but they had to wait almost an hour before they could get their hamburgers at the Lazy Daze Café.

After they ate, they wandered through the town, observing the crowds and noting the measures the shopkeepers had taken to celebrate the opening of the cave the next day. Several display windows were decorated with chalky drawings of cave men dressed in animal skins and carrying clubs. In one picture the cave man dragged a delighted cave woman along by her hair. Several storefronts were decorated with red, white, and blue bunting. In the little park, where the opening ceremonies for the cave man museum would take place the next day, women were hanging paper lanterns from the trees while a man put a fresh coat of white paint on the old-fashioned bandstand. An ice cream vendor did a brisk business from a truck parked near the old train station.

After a while the boys returned to the meadow behind Newt McAfee's house. There was excitement and bustle there too. A tall, stringy man in faded work clothes was stowing a tool kit in the back of a van, muttering to himself as he worked.

"Not right," he declared. "Not right at all. They'll be sorry. You wait and see."

The boys moved closer. They saw built-in cupboards in the van, and a tiny butane stove and a very small refrigerator. There was a bed, neatly made up, and the boys wondered whether this seedy individual lived in the van.

The man scowled at them. "You wouldn't like it if it was you!" he announced.

Just then someone began to shout.

"You're a cretin!" It was James Brandon. He stood outside the little windowless redwood building that had been built against the hillside.

"You get away from here!" yelled Newt McAfee from the doorway of his museum. He had a shotgun in his hands.

Brandon backed away from Newt, clenching his fists. "You should have been locked in a cage at birth!" he told McAfee. "Those bones aren't yours, any more than the rain is yours, or the sun. How dare you surround that hominid with your cornball props!"

"You're trespassing," McAfee said. "You get away from here, and if you want to see that cave man again, you come back tomorrow and pay five dollars, just like anybody else!"

Brandon made a strangled noise and then spun around and stamped away.

McAfee grinned. "Just a little difference of opinion," he told the boys.

"It ain't right!" grumbled the man with the van.

"Well, nobody asked you whether it was right or not," snapped McAfee. "It's no business of yours. Say, boys, you want to come in and have a sneak preview? See my cave man and the museum I built for him?"

He turned back into the small building, and the Three Investigators followed him eagerly. Once they had stepped across the threshold, however, they stopped and gaped.

Newt McAfee had decorated his museum with photographs enlarged into murals —photographs of bones and a skull. Between these rather grisly views were color pictures of more attractive and familiar sights: steam coming from the ground at Lassen, waterfalls tumbling from the cliffs at Yosemite, waves breaking on the coast near Big Sur.

On tables in the center of the room there were models of the California countryside at various stages in its geological history. In one display a glacier covered most of the state. In another the ice had retreated, leaving behind deep valleys and many lakes. There was a model of an Indian encampment with tiny statues of near-naked Indians crouching over fires and preparing ears of corn in various ways. There were also models of prehistoric men fighting a huge mammoth.

"Real classy, isn't it?" said McAfee. "Course, this stuff's all window dressing. The real thing is over there."

Opposite the entrance, four steps led up to a little platform. Beyond the platform there was the bare earth of the hillside and the opening to the cave. Lights shone inside the opening.

Jupiter, Pete, and Bob crossed the museum and went up the steps. They looked into the cave and saw the fossil man.

Jupe drew a quick breath and Bob shuddered.

The cave man was a partial skeleton. Most of the skull was there, brown and hideous. The empty eye sockets stared, and the upper jaw grinned a ghastly grin. There was no lower jaw.

Several ribs remained, jutting from the floor of the cave, and below these were part of a pelvis and some leg bones. The small bones of a hand were quite near the mouth of the cave. They seemed to be reaching for something.

McAfee had had lights installed in the ceiling of the cave, and on the floor near the skull an artificial campfire glowed. Beyond the bones there was a folded Navajo blanket and a basket woven in an Indian design.

The boys instantly sympathized with Brandon's rage. The silliness of the display was sad enough. But much worse, there were footprints all around the bones. The precious fossils had come close to being trampled while someone put in the lights and installed the sham fire.

"I was going to put a pair of moccasins down where his feet would be, if he had feet," said McAfee. "It could look like he'd just kicked 'em off before he laid down to sleep. But then I figured maybe that would be too much."

Bob made a choking sound.

"Probably didn't wear moccasins back in those days—or nothing else, huh?" said McAfee.

The boys didn't answer. They turned away from the cave and went out past a display of shiny key chains and small plastic cave men.

These were for sale, along with T-shirts that had "Citrus Grove, Cradle of Humanity" printed on them.

"We're all set now," said Newt McAfee. He snapped off the lights and locked the door. "John the Gypsy will be on guard here tonight so nobody can get in and mess things up."

"John the Gypsy?" said Jupe.

McAfee nodded toward the thin man who now sat on the bed inside the van.

"That's him. We call him John the Gypsy 'cause he lives in that van, 'stead of having a real home."

McAfee stalked off to his house, and John the Gypsy got out of the van. "Okay," he said. "He wants me to keep watch, I'll keep watch. But that dead one in there ain't going to like it. I sure wouldn't like it if they was coming in to look at me lying there in my bones."

"But he won't know," Pete pointed out. "He's dead, isn't he? Dead people don't know when somebody's looking at them."

"You sure of that?" said John the Gypsy.

A Disturbance
in the Night

Dinner that night was more hamburgers at the Lazy Daze Café. Afterward the boys bought ice cream from the truck near the depot. Then they went back to their loft and lay watching through the window as the sun went down and the moon came up. There was a chill in the air. Wisps of fog floated above the meadow, and the stars winked out. At last the boys pulled their sleeping bags around them and dozed off.

Sometime in the cold dark of the night, Jupe woke to hear the sound of a door opening. Someone had come into the barn—someone who whimpered like a frightened animal.

Jupe sat up and listened.

The whimpering ceased for a moment, then began again.

Pete stirred and sat up. "What's that?" he whispered.

Jupe crept to the top of the ladder and peered down into the blackness below.

"You boys?" croaked a hoarse voice. "Is that you?"

It was John the Gypsy. No sooner had he spoken than he fell, crashing over something in the dark.

Bob yelped with fright, and Pete groped for the flashlight he had left next to his sleeping bag. When he found it, he scrambled to the ladder and flashed the beam down at the barn floor.

John the Gypsy had stumbled into a carton of empty tin cans. Now he lurched to his feet and squinted up at the light. "Is that you?" he cried with panic in his voice. "Answer me, why don't you?"

"It's us," said Jupe. He and Bob and Pete went down the ladder, and John the Gypsy leaned on the fender of Newt's pickup truck and trembled.

"What's the matter?" said Jupe.

"That . . . that dead one!" said John the

Gypsy. "I told you he wasn't going to like all this staring! I told you! Didn't I tell you?"

"What about it?" said Pete. "What happened?"

"He got up and left, that's what he did," John the Gypsy declared. "Serve old Newt right when tomorrow comes and there ain't no bones there! He'll say I took 'em, but he'll be wrong. That one walked away by himself! I seen him go!"

The barn door was open, and the boys looked out and up the slope to the little museum. It was just visible in the moonlight. Its door seemed to be firmly closed.

"You must have had a dream," said Bob gently.

"No." The man shook his head. "I was in my van and I heard a door open. I looked out and there was that cave man. He had a fur over him, like the skin off of something he killed. I could see his eyes. They was terrible—staring straight ahead, and they had a kind of fire in them. And his hair—it was long and raggedy. He went past me and ran straight away across the meadow."

John the Gypsy closed his eyes as if to blot out the memory of the fearful sight.

"We'll go and look," said Jupe.

They walked close together, as if they feared

that it was possible for the prehistoric being in the cave to have gotten up, clothed itself again in flesh and animal skins, and fled across the fields.

But the museum door was locked. When Jupe rattled the knob, Newt McAfee appeared on the porch of his house.

"What's going on there?" cried McAfee. "What you boys doing?"

"Just investigating," Jupe called. "There was some disturbance and your . . . your watchman saw somebody going away across the meadow."

Thalia McAfee appeared on the porch, and Newt stamped down the steps and trudged across the meadow to the museum.

"What happened?" he asked John the Gypsy. "Did that crazy Brandon come snoopin' around?"

"It was the cave man," said John the Gypsy. "He's gone away!"

"What?" McAfee stared in disbelief. Then he raised his voice and shouted, "Thalia! Get my keys!"

Thalia McAfee came running with the keys, and McAfee opened the museum door and snapped on the lights. He strode through the doorway and past the display cases and the models and photo blowups. Lights went on in the underground chamber, and McAfee looked in at his treasure.

The boys peered past McAfee. They saw empty eye sockets looking back at them, and the remains of a grinning mouth. They saw ribs jutting from the smooth-brushed earth, and a hand reaching.

McAfee turned on John the Gypsy. "You're crazy!" he said. "The bones are right here. What's the matter with you?"

"He walked away!" insisted the other. "I seen him go. He was wearing a fur thing like one of them shawls that the Mexican people wear, only fur! And he had hair! He was alive!"

"You shut up!" snapped McAfee. "You want to get the whole town up here?"

He put out the lights in the cave and marched out of the museum. The others followed him.

"Got up and walked, huh?" he said. He made a mocking noise, locked the museum door, and went back to his house. Eleanor was waiting there at the bottom of the porch steps.

"Get inside, Eleanor," commanded McAfee. "It wasn't anything. Crazy John's been seeing things."

He looked back. "John, you keep awake! I ain't payin' you to nap, you know!"

He and Eleanor vanished into the house.

John the Gypsy mumbled something under his breath and took a folding chair out of the van. He placed it halfway between the van and the museum. He then took a shotgun from the van and sat down.

The Three Investigators went back to the loft.

"Must have been a dream," said Pete softly.

"The old guy doesn't seem too bright," said Bob.

"No," Jupe agreed, "but does that mean he sees things that aren't there?"

"Well, no. But anyone can have a dream and not be sure what really happened and what didn't," said Bob.

"He seemed very positive," said Jupe.

"What about the door? It was locked," said Pete.

"Someone could have had a key," said Jupe. He sat up in his sleeping bag and stared out through the window and across the meadow. The trees on the far side of the field were deep black against the night sky, but the grass on the meadow was silver with dew. A series of darker patches crossed that silvery field—a trail that ended in the shadows under the trees.

Had someone walked that way, crushing the grass underfoot and disturbing the droplets of dew?

Jupe started to get up. Then he saw John the

Gypsy rise from his chair and look out across the meadow. John held his shotgun in the crook of his arm, and his head was to one side as if he were listening.

He went to his van after a minute or two and took a blanket from his bed. He wrapped it around himself and sat down again in the chair.

"Perhaps it was a dream," said Jupe softly. "But John the Gypsy believes it was the cave man, and I think he's afraid."

Pete looked nervously out the window at the moonlit meadow. "I don't blame him," he said. "If I saw a cave man wandering around, I'd be terrified!"

A Busy Morning

Jupe was the first one up and out of the barn on Saturday morning. In the bright sunlight the woods did not look particularly dark and mysterious. Jupe began to walk through the meadow toward them. He went slowly, keeping his eyes on the ground, but he didn't see a single footprint. The dark patches that he'd seen in the grass the night before had disappeared with the morning dew.

He had gone perhaps a hundred feet when he spotted a place where the grass was quite thin and the dark earth showed through the green.

He knelt, feeling a shiver of excitement.

He was still there, staring at the ground, when Pete came to his side.

"What is it?" said Pete. "You find something?"

"A footprint," said Jupe. "Someone walked across this field very recently—someone with bare feet!"

Pete crouched to look at the print. Then he stood up and stared at the woods. His face was pale.

"Barefoot?" he said. "On . . . on this rough ground? Does that mean John the Gypsy really saw something?" He looked around.

Jupe said nothing and went on toward the woods. Gulping, Pete followed him. They were alert for further signs of the person who had passed this way, but the grass was long and thick and they reached the edge of the woods without seeing another print.

There was a path under the trees, but the ground there was strewn with pine needles.

"Footprints won't show here," said Jupe, "but maybe farther on . . ."

"Hey, wait a second!" cried Pete. "You don't want to go in there now! I mean, somebody might still be there and . . . and . . . and if we're going to get anything to eat, we'd better get going. There'll be a mob at that café! Come on, or we could wind up starving."

"Pete, this could be important!" said Jupe.

"To who?" retorted Pete. "Hey, come on, Jupe. We can search the woods later."

Reluctantly, Jupe let himself be coaxed away. He and Pete went back to the barn. Bob came out as they arrived. Just then Newt McAfee appeared on his back porch.

"Mornin'," Newt called to the boys. "Beautiful day, ain't it? Ought to get a big turnout for the opening of my museum." He smiled with satisfaction.

"Hey, John!" yelled Newt. John the Gypsy came out of his van holding a bowl of cereal. "Didja see any more cave men last night?" Newt chuckled, but the watchman scowled.

"I seen one, and that's enough," said John, and he disappeared back into his van.

Unperturbed, Newt yelled after him, "Don't you go running off now, John. After breakfast I need your help to fix up a few things in the museum. And then you got to stay here and keep an eye on the place while we have the opening ceremonies in the park."

Newt went back inside the house, and the three boys headed down Main Street for breakfast. Again there was a crowd waiting at the Lazy Daze Café, and by the time they were seated, the boys were famished.

As the waitress took their order, the boys heard the brassy sound of a Sousa march. They looked out past the crowds of pedestrians and lines of cars that inched up the street. A group of very young musicians were rehearsing in the park.

"The band from the local high school," Bob guessed.

The crowd on the sidewalk thinned for a minute, and Jupe and his friends could see the full splendor of red, white, and gold band uniforms. Trucks from several television stations were pulled up on the far side of the park, and a man in a short-sleeved shirt fiddled with the microphone on the bandstand.

The boys were just starting their breakfast when Dr. Terreano came into the café. The immunologist, Hoffer, was with him, sneezing into a handkerchief. The two men glanced down the aisle, and Terreano spotted Jupe and smiled.

"How about making room for them?" said Jupe to his friends.

"Sure," said Pete. "Let's ask them if they want to sit with us."

Jupe went to the front of the café and issued the invitation, and the two scientists accepted gratefully. They followed Jupe to the table.

"Very kind of you boys," said Terreano as he

sat down. His long, almost mournful face was resigned. "This town is a madhouse. I suppose it will be a madhouse until the summer is over and all the tourists go home."

Terreano put a pat of butter on his plate. "We usually have breakfast at the foundation, but Jim Brandon is not very good company today. I understand how he feels, of course. This whole thing has been hard on him."

Elwood Hoffer sneezed and smiled a tight smile. "Hay fever," he explained to the boys. Turning to Dr. Terreano, he said, "It's nice that you're so understanding, Phil, but I personally feel there was no need for Brandon to call you a petrified reactionary."

"Brandon is very high-strung," said Terreano mildly. "Right now he's frustrated. Imagine finding an almost complete fossil skeleton and then not being able to examine it properly. And he wants to see if the find might alter the way we think about the origins of mankind. Not that I think it will—I think the little hominid in the cave is just another evolutionary dead end—but Brandon found it and he should have his chance to evaluate it. I'd be angry, too, if I'd made a major find and things had turned out this way."

"What did Dr. Brandon want to do to the bones?" said Bob. "I've heard about carbon-14 dating."

"That probably wouldn't be useful in this case," said Terreano. "When you use carbon-14 dating, you measure the amount of carbon-14 in your sample. Carbon-14 is a radioactive element, and fifty-seven hundred years after a plant or animal has died, it has just half as many carbon-14 atoms as it did when it was alive. Then, fifty-seven hundred years after that, it has only a quarter as many carbon-14 atoms, and so on and so forth. And after forty thousand years there wouldn't be enough carbon-14 to tell anything."

Bob looked startled. "You think the cave man is older than forty thousand years?"

"I would be astonished if he weren't," said Terreano. "However, carbon-14 dating isn't the only way to find out how old an individual might be. There are other methods of dating, and there are various methods of judging how human a creature might be. We always have trouble with this one, because no one can say with real certainty what makes a human. Is it a matter of a creature walking upright, or is it the size of the brain in relation to the rest of the body, or the teeth . . ."

"Teeth?" echoed Bob. "What about teeth?"

"Human teeth are arranged in the jaw in a sort of arc," said Terreano. "The teeth of other primates, like apes and monkeys, are in a U, with the two sides parallel. There are differences in the size of the molars, too, and . . ."

"And here comes the waitress with our breakfast," said Hoffer. "Thank heavens."

"Sorry," said Terreano. "I didn't mean to bore you, Elwood."

"It was really interesting," Bob declared quickly. "I can see why Dr. Brandon is so mad. If Newt McAfee is tampering with the fossil man . . ."

"And he is," said Terreano. "Not that we're sure it really is a man."

"Don't labor the point, Phil," said Hoffer. "I can't see where a conclusion about it matters to more than a handful of scientists."

Terreano grinned. "Dr. Hoffer's research may be more immediately applied," he told the boys. "If he can prove that heartburn is caused by the body's effort to fight off the common cold, we will all be grateful."

"It's not impossible that heartburn is caused by an immune reaction," Hoffer remarked stiffly. "I'm convinced that breakdowns in our immune system cause many of our troubles, and our genes—what we've inherited—are responsible for very few problems, no matter what Karl Birkensteen might say."

Terreano looked downcast at the mention of the dead geneticist. "A brilliant man," he said seriously. "It was a great loss."

"Perhaps," said Hoffer. "But genetic engineering is at least as risky as splitting atoms. Once you start, where do you stop?"

"Was Dr. Birkensteen actually hoping to improve humans?" said Jupiter. "Eleanor told us yesterday that he had bred smarter chimpanzees. Did he believe he could make smarter men?"

Terreano looked troubled. "I don't think he envisioned anything as radical as a race of super beings, but he did think that too many people are born to live at a very basic level. He felt that man, who has a wonderful brain, should not have to spend twelve to sixteen years in school simply getting the skills to enable him to earn a living."

"Impudence!" said Elwood Hoffer. "Meddling with nature that way can have terrible consequences. Birkensteen's animals are proof of that. He bombarded their sires and dams with various rays, and he saturated them with chemicals. He has been able to train the horses to an extent, and the chimps do have large and nimble brains. However, their life expectancy is only a fraction of what it would be for normal animals in captivity."

"It was as if the animals lived too fast," said Terreano. "At the end Birkensteen was trying to slow down the aging process. He had formulated various mixtures that he gave to the chimps in different ways. He worked with the kinds of chemicals that the brain secretes to prompt sleep or waking.

"His work was very daring and very original. He was in line to get the Spicer Grant, which is money that the board of the Spicer Foundation awards every other year to the scientist in residence whose work may be of greatest benefit to humanity. If Birkensteen had succeeded even partially, he could have had more than a million dollars to use any way he chose."

"What happens now?" asked Pete. "Who'll get the money?"

Terreano shrugged. "Who knows? Dr. Hoffer here might cure all of our stomach ulcers, or Jim Brandon might give us new insights into our origins, or . . ."

"Speaking of Brandon," Hoffer interrupted, "look out there."

They turned toward the windows. They saw Brandon striding along the sidewalk, sidestepping other pedestrians. He was making straight for the café.

Terreano waved when he came in. Brandon took an empty chair from another table and sat down next to Jupe.

"I've got it!" he announced briskly. "I called

Sacramento. I'm going to call back after lunch, at which time the governor will be free to talk."

"The governor will get your hominid out of that cave?" said Terreano.

Hoffer looked at Terreano in surprise. "I thought you two weren't talking."

"That was earlier," said Terreano. "Jim, really, do you think the governor will help?"

"Why not?" said Brandon. "If the state can take property to build roads and schools, why can't it take property in order to save that fossil? I'm going to ask the governor to have the whole area declared a state historical monument. There could easily be more fossils in the hills, and it would be criminal to lose them because McAfee wants to let the public in at five bucks a head!"

Brandon stopped. From the park across the way there came the renewed blare of the band.

"Five of ten," said Hoffer. "The ceremonies are about to start over there, and when they're finished, the mob will march up the road to ogle your cave man. Then they'll no doubt spread out to look for fossils of their own. You're too late, Brandon. It's going to happen, and you can't do a thing to stop it!"

Amazing Events

The ceremonies to open the cave were late in starting. When Brandon, Terreano, and Hoffer reached the park, together with the Three Investigators, Newt McAfee was already seated on the bandstand with Thalia beside him. She wore a black-and-white print dress, and her white gloves came to her elbows. Seated next to the McAfees was a skinny man in a seersucker jacket, who looked wilted in the bright sunshine.

"That's Harry Chenoweth," Terreano whispered to Jupe. "He's the mayor, and he also owns the drugstore. He'll be the master of ceremonies. He loves to make speeches."

A man in a dark suit and a clerical collar joined the McAfees and the mayor. Terreano identified him as the minister of the First Community Church.

Other important townspeople took their places near the minister. Terreano identified the owner of the Happy Hunter Restaurant and the man who ran the motel. The supermarket manager was there. So was the assistant manager, and so was a woman who ran a gift shop on one of the side streets. The owner of the Lazy Daze Café hurried across the street, and the owner of the garage came to sit in the row behind the supermarket manager.

"They've all closed up shop," said Terreano. "The whole town is out here today. The cave man could be a big boost to this town. Most of the businesses have been barely scraping by. Now there's a chance to make some real money. There isn't anybody in town who isn't happy about this."

Jupe looked around the park and saw that almost every civic organization imaginable was represented. There were Campfire Girls and Boy Scouts. There were Shriners, splendid in red fezzes, and Elks, a jovial group identified by a banner. Young men from the Junior Chamber of Commerce wore special ribbons in their lapels, and there were several men in dark suits and white-plumed hats. Mrs. Collinwood appeared in time to identify these as members of the Knights of Columbus.

The ice cream vendor had managed to get his truck close to the park and was doing a brisk business. Next to him was a young man with an immense bunch of helium-filled balloons, surrounded by a group of children.

When it seemed that the park was as crowded as it could possibly be, the mayor got up, tapped at the microphone, then raised his arms to signal silence.

Jupiter glimpsed Eleanor Hess. She was watching, and she wore her usual worried look.

"Okay, everybody!" pleaded the mayor. "Settle down now so Mr. Robertson, from the First Community Church, can ask a blessing on our new enterprise. After that the band from Centerdale High School—let's have a nice hand for the band—they'll lead the parade up the street to the cave man museum. And our own Patty Ferguson—you know her as Miss Avocado at the county fair last year—she'll cut the ribbon to open the cave."

The mayor paused and scanned the crowd. "Where are you, Patty?" he called.

"Here she is!" someone shouted.

The crowd parted and a thin girl with long blonde hair came forward. The crowd cheered as she went up the steps to the bandstand.

Suddenly there was a rushing sound, and the lawn sprinklers in the park turned on!

People gasped and screamed. Some shouted and tried to run. They couldn't. The crowd was too dense.

Jupiter felt the shock of cold water on his face and hands, and then his clothes were wet. He turned his head to exclaim to Pete, but suddenly Pete was collapsing to one side with his eyes closed.

Jupe's knees gave way, and he was no longer standing. He felt himself floating, then dropping as if he were drifting down into the trough of a wave. There wasn't even time to be scared before the darkness overwhelmed him.

Everything was cold. Jupe smelled wet earth. He felt cramped, and something was tickling his nose. He opened his eyes. He was on the ground, his face in the grass. The sprinklers were off.

"What the . . . ?" said a familiar voice.

Jupe hitched himself up on one elbow and saw Brandon. Pete's head was against Brandon's hip.

There were murmurs and cries as a park full

of people tried to get up. The clock in the tower of the Community Church began to strike.

Jupe looked up at the tower and counted the chimes. It was eleven o'clock! Somehow, in some unknown way, he—and the rest of the crowd—had been unconscious for more than forty minutes.

And then it came back to him—the sprinkler system. Someone must have put some chemical into the sprinkler system to make the whole town fall asleep!

Several small children were weeping at the edge of the park, and the balloon vendor was staring up at the sky. The balloons were gone —every one of them.

Jupe managed to stand up. He was giving Bob a hand when John the Gypsy came staggering down the road from McAfee's house.

"The cave man!" shouted John the Gypsy. His voice was hoarser than ususal, and his long arms sawed the air. "He's gone! Somethin' come and took him away!"

Jupe Makes
Deductions

For several hours the field by Newt McAfee's house was a scene of churning activity. Men from the sheriff's department took photographs and dusted the museum for fingerprints. People from the television stations interviewed Newt and Thalia McAfee as the pair spluttered with rage. The television reporters also interviewed James Brandon, who was quite upset, and they talked to the mayor of the town and to several other merchants. The reporters also interviewed John the Gypsy.

"Somethin' come!" John told them. "I was

keepin' watch, just like Mr. Newt said, and I heard this noise behind me, and . . . and I turned around . . ."

He crouched and looked back over his shoulder.

"There was this thing!" he said. "A terrible thing with one big staring eye and . . . and tusks like on an elephant! It wasn't human! Then I was lyin' on the ground, and the door to that museum place was open, and when I looked inside, that poor dead one was gone!"

"The man's been drinking!" said someone in the crowd.

But John had not been drinking, and the cave man was truly gone.

Eventually the television people withdrew, and the sheriff left two men on guard and drove away. The bystanders drifted off. McAfee stood by the barn talking to one of the deputies who had stayed to keep watch. And the Three Investigators, who had been hovering around, walked over to the museum.

"Sorry, boys," said the deputy who stood at the door of the museum. "You can't come in here."

Jupe eyed the door, which was partly open. "The person who stole the bones had a key, didn't he?" he said.

The deputy looked surprised, and he glanced around at the door.

"The door isn't damaged in any way," said Jupe. "Neither is the door frame. If the intruder had had to break in, there would be marks on the door and the frame."

The deputy grinned, then stepped aside. "All right, Sherlock Holmes," he said. "Want to look in here and see what else you can tell me?"

Jupe went into the museum with Pete and Bob.

The small building was orderly except for black smudges where the fingerprint team had been working. Jupe glanced around, then crossed the room and looked into the lighted cavern. The dirt on the floor of the cave was disturbed where the bones had been but was otherwise smooth.

It was then that Jupe noticed a single footprint in the dirt beside the place where the bones had rested. "That print was made by someone wearing rubber-soled shoes," said Jupe. "Newt McAfee wears cowboy boots and John the Gypsy wears laced-up work boots with leather soles. I deduce that since Mr. McAfee and John were the only people who were in here today before the theft, the print was made by the person who took the fossils. The thief wore sneakers or running shoes with a star pattern in the middle of the heel and in the sole."

The deputy nodded. "That's how we see it. A photographer took a shot of that print. We can't go rummaging through closets to find the shoes that made the print, but you never know when a photo will come in handy as evidence."

Jupe took a metal tape measure from his pocket and measured the print. It was twelve inches long.

"A fairly large man," said Jupe.

The deputy grinned. "You're doing okay. Are you going to be a detective someday?"

"I'm a detective *now*," said Jupe. He didn't bother to explain this remark. Instead he looked around, puzzled. "Why?" he said. "That's what I don't understand. Someone went to a lot of trouble. Someone obviously introduced some chemical into the sprinkler system to put the town to sleep . . ."

"That's what we figure," said the deputy. "One of our guys took samples of the water from the sprinklers for testing in the lab. They'll test the water from the reservoir, too, just above town. That's where the water supply comes from."

"It's bizarre," said Jupiter. "Like a science fiction movie. With the town asleep, the thief puts on a frightening disguise and creeps up on John the Gypsy and probably sprays *him* with something that will knock him out. Or perhaps vapors from the sprinklers affect him all the way up here. Then the thief gets into the museum and makes off with the fossils.

"And the question remains, why? Old bones aren't valuable in themselves, like gold or jewelry. And they are important only when linked to the site where they were discovered. The two people most interested in the stolen bones are McAfee and Brandon, and they were both unconscious when the crime took place."

"A weird crime," agreed the deputy. "And we don't even know what to call it. Is it grand larceny, and should squads of men be working on it, running down every lead? Or is it just petty larceny, or even just malicious mischief?"

"Do you think you'll be able to find the thief?" asked Bob.

"Odds are we won't." The deputy looked discouraged. "A lot of thefts never do get solved, you know. There are just too many —and not enough law enforcement people. My guess is that this bone case will go into the crime reports and that'll be the end of it."

The boys stood in gloomy silence.

The deputy moved toward the door. "Okay, you guys. I think you'd better leave now."

The boys obediently filed past him and out onto Newt McAfee's meadow. Over by the barn, Newt and the other deputy had been joined by Thalia, and also by Eleanor, who had evidently just picked up the mail. She was holding a small bundle of letters and a magazine.

Newt McAfee was holding an envelope and a letter. As the Three Investigators drew closer they could see that the writing on the letter had been done in bright green block letters.

Newt was ashy pale. He looked from the letter to the second deputy and then to his wife.

"You . . . you know what it says?" he demanded, his voice thick with fury. "Read this. Just read this!" He held up the letter so everyone could see it. It said:

I HAVE YOUR CAVE MAN AND I WILL KEEP HIM SAFE UNTILL I GET $10,000. IF YOU DO NOT GIVE ME THE MONY I WILL BERY HIM WHERE YOU WILL NEVER FIND HIM. YOU WILL HERE MORE FROM ME.

"Now we know," said Jupe. "We know why somebody stole a bunch of bones—to hold them for ransom!"

The Four-toed
Footprint

"Ten thousand!" cried Eleanor Hess. "That's too much!"

Newt McAfee snorted. "If I catch the guy who did this, I'll fill him full of holes!"

The deputy took the ransom note from McAfee. He glanced at the postmark on the envelope, then read the note again.

"The thief doesn't spell very well," said the deputy. "He's got four words wrong. He does plan ahead, however. This was mailed yesterday in Centerdale."

He put the letter in his pocket. "Mr.

McAfee, who has keys to the museum?"

Newt McAfee took a bunch of keys from his pocket. "I do. This one is it right here," he said. "The only other one's on a board in the kitchen."

Eleanor hurried away to the house, but she was back in a moment to announce that the museum key was missing from the board in the kitchen. "There was a tag on it," said Eleanor. "I guess that's how the thief knew . . ."

"I guess so," said the deputy. "You left your back door open, didn't you? People in this town always leave their doors open. The thief just walked in and picked up the key. Even if you hadn't left the door open, he could have gotten into the kitchen. Anybody could open that old-fashioned door lock with a skeleton key—or even a penknife."

Newt and Thalia McAfee withdrew to their house, completely crestfallen, and Eleanor went with them. The Three Investigators climbed to their loft and sat down near the window. Jupe scowled at his friends.

"I wonder," he said, "who knew about the key in the kitchen?"

"Who knew?" Pete echoed. "Hey, would anyone have to know? Lots of people keep their spare keys in the kitchen, and if the door was so easy to open . . ."

"You're going to say that anyone could have taken the key," said Jupe. "Unfortunately that's true. But there's another thing that makes me wonder. There's the footprint in the cave."

Bob looked surprised. "What about it?" he wanted to know. "It's the thief's print, and he was wearing tennis shoes or running shoes. So what?"

"Remember how the cave looked last night?" said Jupe. "When McAfee first showed us around?"

Pete and Bob both looked puzzled.

"The earth around the bones was all trampled," said Jupe. He shut his eyes as if he were picturing the fossils half-buried in the earth. "Then John the Gypsy had a nightmare in the middle of the night, and he claimed the cave man got up and walked away. Then McAfee opened the museum and we all saw the cave man again. That time, were there footprints?"

Pete and Bob frowned. Then Pete said, "No. No, you're right. But that means . . . that means that McAfee must have tidied up —brushed the earth smooth around the bones."

"We'll see," said Jupe.

He climbed down from the loft and jogged across to the McAfee house and pounded on the door.

Thalia McAfee answered the knock, and then

her husband appeared in the doorway. He and Jupe exchanged a few words.

Jupe turned and hurried back to the barn.

"McAfee says he didn't do any tidying up in the cave," Jupe reported to his friends, "and he says John the Gypsy couldn't have. He never left John alone in there—not even for a minute."

"So that means that during the night, somebody went in there and wiped away those footprints," said Pete. He gulped. "That doesn't make sense. The door was locked. Unless the . . . the cave man *did* get up. But that's impossible!"

"Well, somebody left a footprint in the meadow, at any rate," said Jupe. "I'm going down to the village for a few minutes. I saw a hobby shop yesterday on one of the side streets, and I want to get something there. You stay here and keep your eyes open."

Jupe vanished down the ladder again, and this time he was gone for almost half an hour. When he came back, he had a package. "Plaster of Paris," he said. "I'm going to make a cast of that footprint in the meadow."

He began to rummage among the odds and ends on the workbench in the barn, and soon he had an empty paint can and several pieces of wood of varying lengths.

Jupe poured plaster of Paris into the can and wet it with water from the outside faucet on McAfee's house. Then he stirred it with a stick until it was about as thick as melted ice cream.

"What do you expect to prove with all of this?" asked Pete as the boys set out across the meadow.

"I don't know," said Jupe. "Perhaps nothing. But a barefooted person walked here, and I think we'd better have some proof of it before the footprint gets trampled or blown away in the wind."

When the boys found the footprint again, Jupe knelt and sprayed it with a can of hair spray that he had also bought in town.

"What's the hair spray for?" asked Pete.

"To seal the footprint and keep the plaster from picking up all sorts of dirt and debris," said Jupe.

Next Jupe fashioned a rude frame with four wooden slats from the workbench. He held the pieces of wood together with masking tape and placed the frame around the footprint.

When everything was ready, Jupe carefully poured a layer of plaster of Paris over the footprint. He put a few twigs into the plaster to reinforce the cast and waited for the first plaster layer to harden slightly. Then he poured again.

"Good work!" said Pete.

"It's too bad we don't have a client to appreciate all of this," said Bob. "Do you suppose Newt McAfee would like to hire us?"

"Do you suppose The Three Investigators would like him as a client?" Jupe countered.

"No, sir!" said Pete vehemently. "He is one mean guy, and I don't like his wife either. I don't know how Eleanor Hess stands those two."

Jupiter sighed. "The woman who owns the hobby shop knew Eleanor's mother," he said. "Mrs. Hess was pretty, and the woman thinks Thalia McAfee was jealous of her. She hinted that Thalia takes it out on Eleanor. She said right out that Newt is so stingy he makes Eleanor pay for her room and board, and he's made her pay ever since her parents died."

Bob looked startled. "But she was only eight! How could she pay? Did her parents leave money?"

"They owned a house in Hollywood," said Jupe. "McAfee rents it and collects the rent."

"Oh," said Bob. "And you got the hobby shop lady to tell you all that? How'd you manage that?"

"I mentioned that we were camping in McAfee's barn, and she wanted to know how much he was charging. When I told her, she just shook her head and started to talk. She also told me that John the Gypsy can't read or write. He supports himself with odd jobs, and she thinks Newt cheats him because he has trouble keeping track of the time he spends working for Newt."

"Well, so much for John the Gypsy," said Bob. "If he can't write, he couldn't have sent the ransom note."

"He could be an accomplice, but somehow I don't think he is," said Jupe. "He isn't really bright enough to be taken into anyone's confidence. And I think he wasn't acting this morning. He was really afraid. So let's eliminate him. The case could be involved enough without him."

"So we *are* taking the case, huh?" said Pete. "Who's our client? Eleanor?"

"Do we have to have a client?" asked Jupe. "Isn't the puzzle fascinating enough by itself? A fossil man, dead for ages, was stolen, and the thief was able to introduce something into the sprinkler system so that an entire town went to sleep."

Bob grinned. "It's so crazy that I love it." He sat down on the ground, took a pad from his pocket, produced a ballpoint pen, and began to write.

"A missing cave man," he said. "Some mysterious drug in the water system. A ransom note that's poorly spelled, and that may not even be important. The spelling, I mean. It could be faked. And that brings us to the suspects."

Bob looked up at his friends. "Brandon?" he said. "He wanted the bones out of the cave, and he could have sent the ransom note to cover up."

"He was asleep in the park when the bones were swiped," Pete pointed out. "I woke up leaning on him. Hey, everybody in town was asleep in the park. We don't have any suspects!"

"We don't know for sure that *everyone* in the town was at the ceremony," said Jupe. "And anyway, the kidnapper may have had some way to avoid the effect of the substance in the sprinklers. If that's the case, anyone in town could be a suspect."

"Careful," said Bob. "Here comes Eleanor."

Jupe looked around and saw Eleanor Hess coming across the grass. Quickly Jupe shifted so that he sat between Eleanor and the plaster cast in the ground. "Hi," he said when Eleanor was fairly close. "We were just . . . just talking about all the strange things that happened today."

Eleanor nodded, and after she hesitated for a moment as if she were unsure of her welcome, she sat down facing the Investigators. "I . . . uh . . . I'm going up to the foundation now, and I thought maybe you'd like to . . . to come along."

"That would be very nice," said Jupe, "and we'd . . ."

"You don't have to," said Eleanor. "I just thought if you have nothing to do." Suddenly she blurted out, "Ten thousand dollars! That's an awful lot of money! Uncle Newt's gone to talk to some other people in town about getting it together and . . . and it's getting to be such a big deal!"

And Eleanor burst into tears.

"Hey, it's not that bad," said Bob. "I mean, the cave man is just a bunch of bones. It isn't as if somebody were holding a real live person for ransom, is it?"

"No. But my uncle's as mad as if it were. He's so mad he scares me. He says he's losing money every second the cave man is gone. I guess he is. The cave man could have paid much better than the hardware store. Things can get slow at the store."

"Do you help out there?" asked Jupe.

Eleanor nodded. "When I'm not at the foundation. But I'd rather be at the foundation. Nobody yells there except Dr. Brandon, and he doesn't really mean it." She smiled suddenly, and her cheeks became quite pink. "Dr. Brandon is kind. He says I should go to college—San

Diego State or one of those schools."

"Why don't you?" Bob asked.

"Well, I'd need one of the cars to get there, and Aunt Thalia says no. She says it's a waste of money to send a girl to college, and besides I shouldn't forget what class I come from."

"What does that mean?" Pete asked.

"I guess it means I'll be getting uppity if I go to college," said Eleanor. "Aunt Thalia says my mother got uppity and she thought she was too good for this little town, so she went off and married my father, and look what happened."

Eleanor stopped. Her face went grim and hard. "She gives me a swift pain!" she announced. "My mother could have been in an auto accident anywhere. You don't have to be wicked or stuck up to get hit by a bus in an intersection. My mother was nice. She had pretty hair. My father was nice too. He played the oboe for the Los Angeles Philharmonic, and I remember him practicing. The oboe is really a wonderful instrument. We don't have any music in the house now—except on radio and TV."

She stopped again, then burst out, "I want to get away! I'm saving all I can. I have over a hundred dollars saved from my job at the foundation. Uncle Newt and Aunt Thalia use the rent from my parents' house in Hollywood to pay my expenses, but the foundation money is mine!"

"Have you asked your uncle and aunt about the rent money?" said Jupe. "If you left here, they wouldn't need it for your expenses, would they?"

She looked startled. "But I couldn't do that! They'd be furious! They'd throw me out."

"So what?" said Pete. "You want to leave anyway."

"But I don't have anyplace to go!"

"You could go to the house in Hollywood," Bob suggested.

"No, I couldn't. People live there."

She got up. "I'm saving," she said. "When I have enough, I'll leave. Are you coming up to the foundation with me?"

"We'll be right along," said Jupe. "There's something we have to do at the barn first."

The boys watched her go.

"Do you suppose she'll ever get away?" said Pete.

"I don't know," said Jupe. "She doesn't want to be here, but she's afraid to be anyplace else."

Jupe turned his attention to the plaster cast. The plaster was set now, and when it was lifted from the earth, it presented the mold of a bare right foot.

"Beautiful!" exclaimed Pete.

"Hmm, the wandering cave man had trouble with his foot," said Jupe. "Look. You can see the big toe, then a space, and then three smaller toes. It looks as if the second toe got squeezed up so that it didn't leave an imprint on the ground."

"A hammer toe!" said Bob. "On a cave man?"

"Seems unlikely, doesn't it?" said Jupe. "Foot problems usually come with shoes that don't fit."

Jupe took his tape measure out and measured the print. It was barely nine inches long.

"The thief who left his shoe print in the museum was a large person," said Jupe. "The barefoot wanderer was small."

Pete gulped. "Could it have been the cave man?"

"The cave man is dead," Jupe said. "He's been dead for ages, and dead people do not get up and walk. Our criminal could be almost anyone—anyone at all. But it is not a dead man!"

11

The Missing Pages

The boys found Eleanor Hess in the stable grooming the horse that had been Dr. Birkensteen's special charge. Frank DiStefano was there, too, leaning on a stall and watching.

"Hear the cave man's come up missing," he said. "Just my luck I missed it. I was home with stomach flu."

"That's too bad," said Jupe. "You okay now?"

"Oh, yeah. Fine. That stuff never lasts long."

"It was really weird in the park," said Pete. "Everyone just went to sleep."

"Figures!" said DiStefano. "That's what usu-

91

ally happens around here. Nap time!" He glanced at Eleanor and said, "Take it easy. Don't race your motor." Then he went out, silent on rubber-soled shoes.

Pete stared after him. "He's wearing running shoes," Pete observed.

"Lots of people wear running shoes," said Eleanor.

She had finished grooming the horse. She let it out into the enclosure next to the stable, put away the grooming things, and started toward the house.

The boys went along with her into the workroom that had been used by Birkensteen. The chimpanzees leaped about in their cage when they saw her, screaming with delight.

"Okay! Okay!" Eleanor laughed and opened the cage, and the chimps frolicked around her.

"Too bad they don't like you," said Pete.

Eleanor smiled. "They're sweet, aren't they? And they do like me, but they miss Dr. Birkensteen."

"It would be odd if they didn't," said Bob.

Jupe said nothing. He was standing next to the dead scientist's desk, his eye caught by the appointment book there. He opened the book and idly flipped the pages, then suddenly came to attention.

Next to the page for April 28, and on the right-hand side of the book, was the page for May 19.

"More than half the pages for May are missing from Dr. Birkensteen's calendar," announced Jupe. He frowned. "That's interesting! Wasn't it in early May that he died? I remember that it was one of those foggy, cold days we get in the springtime."

Eleanor sat very still, her faced turned away from Jupiter. "It was . . . it was sometime in May," she said in a low voice.

"Why would he tear the pages out of his calendar?" wondered Jupe.

"I . . . I don't know, really," she said. She was holding one of the chimps in her arms, rocking it back and forth as if it were a child. Bob and Pete watched, alert and curious.

"You went with Dr. Birkensteen to Rocky Beach," said Jupe. "The day he died. Could the missing pages have something to do with that?"

"No," she said. "No, I . . . I don't suppose so."

"Did the trip have anything to do with the chimps?" Jupe persisted.

"Maybe. I suppose it could have. I didn't really know much about his work. I only helped

with the animals, and I went with him because
. . . because he was nice and he didn't feel
well."

"What address on Harborview Lane were
you looking for? And who lived there?" Jupe
pressed on.

Eleanor looked worried and nervous. She
cleared her throat and ducked her head, and
the boys saw a tear run down her cheek.

"I'm not doing too well today," she said. "I'm
sorry. Maybe you'd better go."

The boys left. In the hallway outside the
workroom they met Mrs. Collinwood. She had
on a ruffled apron over her print dress, and she
wore a dark wig with a white streak in it.

"Everything all right?" she said, smiling
brightly.

It struck Jupe that Mrs. Collinwood was a bit
of a busybody—and might know useful things.
Jupe allowed his face to settle into a mournful
expression. "I'm afraid we've upset Eleanor,"
he said. "I mentioned Dr. Birkensteen to her.
She's crying."

"Tch!" Mrs. Collinwood shook her head.
"She was fond of him. But then, we were all
fond of him. He was one of the nicest people
here."

"Do you know why he went to Los Angeles

that day?" said Jupe. "The day he died? Did he have friends there?"

"I don't know. He wasn't one for much talk. I suppose it had something to do with those animals. You can't imagine how he fussed over them. You'd think he was raising children and getting them ready for college. And whenever one of them died, he'd carry on as if he'd lost his best friend."

"A lot of them died?" said Jupe.

"Yes. And he'd do autopsies to see why. Sometimes he did operations when they were alive too. And sometimes when they were sleeping, he'd just stand and watch them."

She looked thoughtful. "They used to sleep so much. They seem livelier now."

There was a thump and a crash from a room down the hall.

"Oh, dear!" said Mrs. Collinwood. She hurried to an open doorway. "Frank, try to be more careful."

Frank DiStefano came out. He had a broom in one hand and two pieces of a white dish of some kind in the other. "No real harm done," he said in his insolent way. "It was empty."

"The next time it might not be," she said.

He ignored this and went on, nodding to the boys.

"When are you going to get those things from the market?" Mrs. Collinwood called after him.

"For Pete's sake, I'm going now!" he cried. "What do you want from me, anyway?"

Mrs. Collinwood made an exasperated noise as he disappeared through a door at the end of the hall.

When the boys went out through the front of the house, they saw DiStefano getting into an old two-door sedan that was parked in the drive. He started the engine, then waited for them to reach the driveway.

"Got to keep these women in their place," he said. He gave a cocky grin and offered them a lift.

The boys looked at the back seat and saw a jumble of magazines, muddy boots, a crushed box of tissues, a scuba mask, and a wet suit.

"Thanks anyway," said Jupe. "We're only going to the bottom of the hill."

DiStefano nodded and the car spurted away.

"He's got a big mouth," said Pete.

Jupe only said, "Um!" for he was musing on the conversation he had just had with Mrs. Collinwood.

"I wish Dr. Birkensteen hadn't been so reserved," he said at last. "If he had told Mrs. Collinwood more about his mysterious errand in Rocky Beach, I'm sure she would have talked of it just now. She isn't a deceitful or secretive person—which I think is more than we can say for Eleanor Hess. I'm sure Eleanor is lying to us. But why? What is she concealing?"

"Something about the cave man?" Bob ventured.

"Who knows?" sighed Jupe.

When the Three Investigators reached Newt McAfee's meadow, they spotted Thalia McAfee out on the back porch. "Have you seen Eleanor?" she called.

"She's up at the foundation," Bob called back.

"Hmph!" said Thalia. "Fussing with those animals again! She'd bring them here if I'd let her, but I told her there ain't nobody stays in this house that don't pay rent."

"No, ma'am," said Jupe. "By the way, one of the deputies told us earlier that the water from the sprinkler system was being tested. Do you know if they found anything in it?"

"They didn't," said Thalia. "One of the sheriff's men called a while ago. There was nothing in the sprinklers and nothing in the reservoir where the water comes from. The sheriff thinks the whole town's suffering from mass hypnosis!"

A Noise
in the Ruins

Jupe sighed as Thalia McAfee went back inside. "I can't believe in mass hypnosis," he said to his fellow investigators. "Also, I keep being disturbed at the thought of that dead scientist."

"I always find dead people disturbing," Pete declared.

"That isn't what I mean," said Jupe. "I was referring to the pages missing from the appointment calendar. Surely they are significant. I'd like an opportunity to go through Dr. Birkensteen's papers. I wonder if that could be arranged."

"I'll bet it couldn't," Bob predicted. "If his work was so important, those papers are probably locked up in a safe someplace."

"Hm," said Jupe. His tone was grim. But then he brightened again. "How interesting that Frank DiStefano wasn't in the park this morning," he said. "I wonder who else was missing when the cave man was kidnapped."

Bob frowned. "Everybody we know was there, except DiStefano and . . . and John the Gypsy."

Pete grinned. "Hey!" he said. "How about John the Gypsy? We shouldn't forget him just because he acts like a dimwit. Maybe that's just an act, and he's really sort of brainy."

"That doesn't make sense," said Bob. "He's been here for years and years, hasn't he? If he were smart, he'd have tipped his mitt long ago."

"So he isn't smart," said Jupe. "Probably he isn't even reasonably cunning. But last night he saw a cave man walk, and we have a plaster cast of that cave man's footprint. Where did the cave man go?"

Pete looked toward the woods beyond the meadow. "Okay," he said. "Let's go see where."

The Three Investigators went first to the place where Jupiter had taken a cast of the footprint. Then they walked slowly on. They found no more prints until they were in under the trees. There was one low-lying spot where the earth was bare, and, sure enough, the shoeless wanderer had come that way. Pete pointed to the print. The Three Investigators skirted it and pushed on without a sound, moving stealthily as if someone might be lurking behind a tree, waiting to strike down a pursuer.

Finally the trees thinned, and beyond them was a clearing. The boys stood at the edge of the wood and looked out at grass and at brambles that surrounded the crumbling remains of an old building. It had walls of brick that were broken in several places and a red tile roof that had fallen in here and there, so that some of the supporting beams could be seen.

"Once upon a time," Bob observed, "I think that must have been a church."

No one answered him, and the three boys crossed the clearing.

Two great wooden doors had once closed the entrance of the church, but one of them had fallen off its hinges. It lay inside on the tile floor. The boys stepped over it as they entered the building.

"Do you suppose the barefoot cave man came in here last night?" said Pete. He looked around nervously.

"No way of telling," said Jupe. "He wouldn't leave any traces on this floor."

Bob made a hesitant movement toward the front of the church. Two steps there led up to a place that was higher than the area where the boys stood.

"If there was an altar," said Bob, "it would have been up there. And look. There's a doorway that must lead into another room. Maybe it was a vestry where the priest or the minister could put on his robes."

The Three Investigators waited in the silence, each one somehow unwilling to cross the church and go up the two steps and open the door to the hidden room.

Suddenly they heard a sound that made their hearts beat faster.

Someone was moving behind the closed door! There was a creaking and a rustling, and something fell clattering to the tiles.

Then there was stillness.

Pete stepped backward, as if he might run.

Bob made a move toward the closed door, and Pete caught his arm.

"Don't!" whispered Pete. "Suppose it's . . . *him*?"

He didn't explain. He didn't have to. The other two understood. Suppose the cave man had walked again. Suppose he had escaped from the captor who held him for ransom, and the long-dead bones had somehow assumed flesh once more, and the ancient creature was there, crouched in the hidden room, armed!

Armed? With what?

"Impossible!" said Jupiter bravely. He ran forward and went up the two steps. As he did so, there was another noise—a noise as if something had touched the door, rattling it slightly.

Jupe put his hand on the doorknob, and then he froze. A prickle of horror stirred his scalp.

The knob was turning under his hand. It was turning by itself! Then the old hinges groaned in protest, and the door began to open!

Another Theft

"Good night!" exclaimed Dr. Hoffer, his hand still on the knob of the vestry door. "You startled me. I didn't know anyone was here."

Jupiter was still trembling, but he managed to smile. "We were exploring," he said.

Hoffer walked through the vestry door into the church. The boys could see that there was a small room behind him, with a door leading to the outside.

"You boys want to be careful," said Hoffer. "This is private property. It belongs to the Lewison family. They own a big house on the far side of the hill. I have permission to come here, but I don't think they like strangers."

He sat down on the steps that separated the altar area from the rest of the church. "It's amazing how things never really change," he said. "There is an empty building in the neighborhood, and I find you three exploring it. I would have done the same thing when I was a youngster. When I was your age, there was a vacant house in our neighborhood in Milwaukee. We found an unlocked window and we got in and established a clubhouse in the cellar. It was very pleasant there—not infested with people like parents and teachers."

Dr. Hoffer stopped and sneezed. He took out a handkerchief and dabbed at his eyes.

"It's that hay fever again," he said. "I'm always having allergic reactions to things. It's what prompted my interest in immunity."

He stood up. "This is as far as I'll go today," he said. "Something in the air isn't agreeing with me. Are you boys coming back to the village? If I were you, I don't think I'd explore further. Edward Lewison has been known to take a shotgun to trespassers."

"Like somebody else we know," said Jupe. "Newt McAfee."

"Then let's go back to the village," said Pete.

The boys followed Dr. Hoffer out through the vestry.

"You're interested in allergies?" said Jupe as they plunged into the woods. "But you became an immunologist. I thought people who took care of allergies were allergists."

"They are," said Hoffer. "However, one thing leads to another. An immunity is a sort of allergic reaction."

"It is?" said Bob.

Hoffer nodded. "Our bodies have various ways of defending themselves. They can produce things called antibodies. The antibodies destroy invading viruses and bacteria, or they cancel the poisons that come from the tiny invaders. If you get German measles, for example, your body will produce antibodies to fight the disease. Once that happens, you won't get the disease again because the antibodies remain in your system. So we say that you're immune to German measles.

"Now suppose your body produces antibodies in reaction to things that don't bother most people. Say you're allergic to a certain pollen. Your body will produce antibodies that react with the pollen, and it will release a chemical compound called histamine. This makes your nose swell and your eyes water.

"So our immune system saves our lives when it fights disease, but it can make our lives miserable when it gets out of control. I believe that many more human ills are due to breakdowns of the immune system than is commonly thought.

"Suppose a person's body produces chemicals that make his joints swell up, the way the mucus membranes of the nose swell up when a patient has hay fever. Arthritis, eh? Why wouldn't that be an allergic reaction? And cancer? There's a virus theory of cancer. Why not an allergy theory? Cancer consists of cells growing out of control, possibly in response to something harmful. And crime!"

"Crime?" echoed Pete.

"Crime can be a reaction to a threat," said Dr. Hoffer. "Imagine a person growing up in a dangerous place. To protect himself, the person develops a reaction to the approach of any stranger—a violent reaction. Without even thinking, he will attack before he can be attacked. The defenses have run wild."

Dr. Hoffer looked grim. "The defense system is our greatest asset, and our greatest threat too. I have rats in the laboratory that live sealed behind glass partitions, protected from infection. I have been able to short-circuit their immune systems, and they will live much longer than unprotected rats. Of course, they are especially open to disease because they have no defenses. But if I could learn to modify their reactions, to regulate their immunities, they could exist outside the glass cages and still avoid many of the ills that kill their fellows.

"Now imagine what controlled immunities could mean to humans. Think of a world without all those terrible diseases!"

Hoffer nodded. "Worth any effort!" he said. "What Birkensteen was doing with intelligence was completely visionary, and probably dangerous as well. And Brandon is a child playing with dusty bones. What I am doing is practical, and it could have tremendous impact almost immediately."

They had reached the field behind the McAfee house. Hoffer paused to shake hands with the boys. Then he went on to the road and up the hill toward the foundation.

There was a stunned silence as he left. Then Pete said, "Okay. I'm convinced. I nominate Dr. Hoffer for the million dollars from the Spicer Grant."

Jupe just nodded, and the boys went on down the street to the café.

The crowd in the town was thinning out now, and there was no long wait for a table. The boys ate an early dinner, talking quietly among themselves about the events of the day.

"A weird case," was Pete's conclusion. "Really squirrelly. The whole town falls over in a dead sleep, and a cave man takes a stroll."

"And we have the cave man's footprint, if that's who it was," said Jupe. "What can we learn from it? What would you think of showing it to Dr. Brandon? He's used to deducing things from clues like a bit of bone or a footprint preserved in mud. If there could be a connection between the footprint on the meadow and the cave man, he would recognize it instantly."

"Jupe, it couldn't be the cave man," said Bob.

"Perhaps not, but there *was* a barefooted person on the meadow, and John the Gypsy swears he saw a cave man, and Dr. Brandon certainly would be interested to know that, wouldn't he?"

"Okay," said Bob. "I guess it's worth a try."

The boys finished their meal and hurried up the street to the barn, where they took the cast of the footprint from Jupe's sleeping bag. Then they went on to the Spicer Foundation. They found James Brandon in his workroom.

Brandon was sitting at a desk strewn with papers and books. He glared at the Three Investigators when they came in. The boys almost feared that he was about to fly into one of his shouting rages. However, once he closed the book he was reading, they could see that he was not really angry, just deeply involved with what he was doing.

"Well?" he said. "What is it?"

"We want some advice," said Jupiter, "and perhaps some information. Dr. Brandon, we have been staying in the loft in Newt McAfee's barn, and we can see the museum from the window there. Last night, very late, there was a disturbance there."

Jupe went on to tell of John the Gypsy's strange experience and of finding the footprint on the meadow. Then he showed the cast of the footprint to Brandon.

"Of course, it is impossible to believe that the cave man walked in the meadow," said Jupiter. "But someone did, and you are accustomed to deducing facts about a person with far less evidence than this."

Brandon smiled. "When you talk that way, I get the feeling that I have been marooned in a nineteenth-century detective story." He put the cast on his desk. "Well, if you were hoping for a prehistoric creature, this isn't it," he said. "The person who made this footprint is used to wearing shoes. When a person goes barefoot all the time, the feet spread and the toes splay out. But the person who made these prints had narrow feet. Also, he has a hammer toe, which is unlikely for someone who doesn't wear shoes."

"John the Gypsy said it was a cave man, though," said Bob. "He said it had long shaggy hair and was wearing an animal skin."

James Brandon chuckled. "Do you really suppose that prehumans wore clothes? I don't know what John the Gypsy thinks he saw, but the person who made this print is not the cave man. Not only are the feet too narrow—even assuming that a dead hominid could wander around—but the feet are too big."

"Too big?" Pete looked startled. "But they're small! Only nine inches."

"Primitive beings were very small," said Brandon. "I took measurements of the fossil in the cave, and from the size of the bones, I would say that our cave man was about ninety-five centimeters tall when he was up and walking around. That isn't much more than three feet. The individual who made this footprint had to be at least five three or four."

Brandon went to a cabinet that stood against the wall. "When I was in Africa," he said, "I was fortunate enough to find an almost complete fossil skeleton that dates back almost two million years. It is slightly smaller than the Citrus Grove hominid, but it will give you an idea."

Brandon unlocked the double doors of the cabinet and swung them wide.

Then he stood as if frozen, gaping at the empty shelves in front of him.

"It's gone!" he said in a whisper.

Then, taking a deep breath, he shouted, "Gone! It's gone! Someone's stolen my hominid!"

The Dead Man's Notes

Jupiter won a small victory over Newt McAfee that evening. He announced that since so many of the tourists who had come to Citrus Grove for the opening of the cave were gone, he and his friends would move from the loft to the campground. McAfee hastily lowered his fee from ten dollars to three, and the boys paid the money and retired to the loft chuckling.

For a while they lay in the darkness, pondering the events of the day. At last Pete said, "It's wild. Open season on old bones."

"I wonder when Dr. Brandon's fossils were

taken," said Bob. "He said he's been so busy with other things that he hasn't looked at them for two or three months."

"That would put it back in the spring," said Jupe, "about the time Dr. Birkensteen died."

Pete groaned. "Not that again. Birkensteen had nothing to do with fossils. There's no connection, except that he lived here."

"There's Eleanor Hess," said Jupe. "Is she lying about that trip to Rocky Beach? She knew they were looking for an address on Harborview Lane. Wouldn't it be logical for her to know what the exact address was and who lived there?"

"True," said Bob. "And she won't look right at you when she talks about it."

"And why are the pages missing from Birkensteen's calendar?" Jupe persisted. "What notations did Birkensteen make on those pages? Did he tear out the pages himself, or did someone else?"

"Hey!" Pete sat up in his sleeping bag. "Suppose Birkensteen was in touch with someone in Rocky Beach, and he just happened to mention the cave man. Couldn't he have planted the idea of the theft there? We've been acting like someone in Citrus Grove had to be the thief, but maybe that isn't true. The town was crawling with visitors today!"

"That might be possible," said Jupe, "except Brandon didn't discover the cave man until *after* Birkensteen died."

"Oh," said Pete.

"There still could be some connection, though," said Jupe. "Maybe just less direct. If we only had those missing calendar pages. And Birkensteen's notes. The notes on his work in the last days might have a clue."

"Or there might be a clue in Rocky Beach," said Bob. "You said Birkensteen was looking for Harborview Lane. I know that street. It's a short dead-end street off Sunset. Suppose I go to Harborview and ring doorbells and say that Dr. Birkensteen's briefcase is missing, and ask if he left it when he came in May. Of course, he never got where he was going, but I sure ought to get a reaction if someone from Harborview Lane knew him. I'll take the early bus in the morning. I can be in Rocky Beach in a couple of hours."

"Very well," said Jupe. "I'll go back to the foundation to see if I can find Dr. Birkensteen's papers. Dr. Brandon might help me. He seemed friendly enough this evening."

"And I'll go to Centerdale," Pete decided.

"What's in Centerdale?" asked Bob.

"I don't know for sure," said Pete, "but it's the next town down the road, and that's where the ransom note for the cave man was mailed. Maybe I can pick up some clues there."

"Good enough," said Jupe. He closed his eyes and listened to the clock in the church tower down the road begin to strike the hour. He began to count the strokes, but didn't finish. He dropped off to sleep, and it seemed only a minute later that he woke to find Pete shaking him.

"It's almost eight," said Pete. "Let's go!"

Bob was already up. Jupe and Pete joined him at the outside faucet, and the three washed, shivering in the chill air.

The boys ate a hearty breakfast at the café on the main street, and then they separated. Jupe went up the road to the Spicer Foundation.

The front door of the big house was open, and he could hear Mrs. Collinwood inside.

"I could swear it wasn't there yesterday," said Mrs. Collinwood. "I looked and looked."

Jupe peeped through the door. Mrs. Collinwood was in the living room. This morning she wore a brown wig that fell almost to her shoulders.

"I told you it would turn up," said a second woman. She was dressed in a blue uniform and a white apron. She had a feather duster in her hand, and she stood and watched Mrs. Collinwood adjust her wig in front of a mirror. "You mislaid it, that's all," she said.

"It wasn't there!" insisted Mrs. Collinwood. "You don't just mislay a wig!"

The woman trailed away with her duster, and Mrs. Collinwood noticed Jupe hovering in the doorway.

"If you've come to see Eleanor, she's not here yet," said Mrs. Collinwood.

"Is Dr. Brandon in?" Jupe asked.

"He is, if you've got the gumption to face him," said Mrs. Collinwood. "You know where his room is."

Jupe thanked her and went through the living room and into the hall. Even before he reached Brandon's workroom, he could hear the archaeologist. Brandon was shouting, and there were bumps and crashes. It sounded as if he were throwing things.

Jupe hesitated in front of the workroom door, wondering whether he dared to knock.

Suddenly the door was snatched open. "What is it?" shouted Brandon when he saw Jupe. "What do you want?"

"Don't take the boy's head off," said a second person. It was Terreano, sitting quietly in an armchair near Brandon's desk.

Brandon opened his mouth as if to shout again, but suddenly he smiled. "I'm sorry," he said. "Come on in."

Jupe entered the workroom. He saw books and papers scattered on the floor, and the typewriter table upset.

Terreano smiled at him. "Excuse the mess. Dr. Brandon was giving vent to some strong feelings."

Brandon flushed and looked embarrassed. He picked up the typewriter table and set it in place next to the desk. Then he picked up the typewriter. The roller dropped to the floor and bounced away.

"Oh, blast!" cried Brandon.

"Dr. Brandon never actually strikes anyone," said Terreano, "but he's very hard on the furniture."

"Who wouldn't be mad?" demanded Brandon. "That butterball McAfee is saying I stole his cave man to keep the sightseers from trampling it, and then I sent a ransom note so it would look as if somebody else did it. Then, according to him, I hid the fossil bones I had here so it would look like some kind of nut was running around taking bones."

Brandon glared at Jupe. "McAfee had the gall to telephone and say that. I may kill him!"

"Jim, nobody seriously believes that you stole anything," said Terreano. "McAfee is sore because his cave man is gone. He's striking out blindly."

"Dr. Brandon, isn't it curious that your fossils were also stolen?" said Jupe.

"It isn't curious," snapped Brandon. "It stinks!"

"But is it likely that a second thief is involved?" said Jupe. "Let's assume that the same person who took your hominid from the cabinet also took the cave man. Who knew about the hominid in the cabinet?"

Brandon was suddenly attentive. "My gosh! You're right! Its presence in Citrus Grove wasn't publicized. Well, the people at the foundation knew. Mrs. Collinwood. Dr. Terreano here."

"What about Eleanor Hess?" said Jupe.

"That scared little rabbit of a girl?" said Brandon. "She wouldn't have the nerve to steal even if she knew about my hominid. And yet . . . yet I think she watches me. I've caught her staring at me. She peeks out from behind the furniture. It's very strange."

Terreano laughed. "Didn't you know?" he said. "She's got a crush on you. She has all the symptoms. She bumps into things when you're around, and she drops things. She's very young. It's just a nice schoolgirl crush."

"Oh, blast!" said Brandon. He had gone rather red.

"Eleanor Hess is in an intriguing position,"

said Jupiter. "She's familiar with the doings of the people here, and she knows everything about the McAfee house."

Brandon looked narrowly at Jupe. "Just why are you so interested?" he asked.

"My friends and I are detectives," said Jupe.

"Detectives?" Brandon chuckled.

"Yes," said Jupe, pulling a small card out of his pocket and handing it to Brandon. It read:

THE THREE INVESTIGATORS
"We Investigate Anything"
? ? ?

First Investigator	Jupiter Jones
Second Investigator	Peter Crenshaw
Records and Research	Bob Andrews

"Very impressive," said Brandon, passing the card to Terreano and winking at him.

"We are not amateurs, Mr. Brandon," said Jupe with great dignity. "We have solved puzzles that have baffled sleuths far older than ourselves. Usually we act on behalf of a client. This time, however, we have no client. But the riddle of a kidnapped cave man is unique. We are most anxious to find out what really happened."

"That makes two of us," said Brandon sincerely. "All right, my curious young friend, I agree that Eleanor Hess is in an interesting position. She is Newt McAfee's niece, and also an employee here. But she doesn't have the nerve to pull off a theft."

"She was very friendly with Dr. Birkensteen," said Jupe. "Could there be some connection between the theft of the cave man and Dr. Birkensteen's trip to Rocky Beach?"

"When he died?" said Terreano. "But that was almost three months ago! Before the cave man was even discovered!"

"Even so," said Jupiter, "do you know why Dr. Birkensteen went to Rocky Beach?"

Brandon scowled. "No. He didn't confide in any of us."

"I think Eleanor knows," said Jupe, "but she doesn't confide in anyone either. There are pages missing from Dr. Birkensteen's appointment book. They are the pages for the end of April and the beginning of May. I was wondering if I might look at his notes for those days. They might hold some clue."

Brandon looked at Terreano, and then he nodded. "Everything is still in Birkensteen's room," he told Jupiter. "His papers haven't been disturbed."

The three left Brandon's workroom and went down the corridor to Birkensteen's laboratory.

There were sheaves of notes. They were

neatly arranged in loose-leaf folders marked
"Reaction Times" and "Manual Dexterity" and
"Communications Skills." There were notebooks having to do with chemical stimulation
and with X-ray exposure times, and there were
headings that Jupe could not even begin to
comprehend.

"It would take another geneticist to explain
it," said Terreano.

Jupe nodded. "Still," he said, "there might
be something. And remote as it might seem,
there may be a connection with the cave man."

There was silence in the laboratory after that
as Jupe and Brandon and Terreano leafed
through the notebooks. After a while Jupe said,
"There are no notes for experiments after April
tenth."

Brandon flipped to the back of the book he
held. "You're right," he said. "The last notes in
this one are for March twenty-fifth."

They took down book after book and looked
at the last entries. There were no notations
made after the first days of April.

"But he didn't stop work," said Brandon. "He
worked every day. And he was very methodical.
He would have made notes. What happened to
them?"

"The same thing that happened to the pages
from his calendar," said Jupiter.

There was a small stack of magazines on the workbench, and Jupe picked one up and leafed through it. Someone had inserted a slip of paper halfway through to mark a place. The magazine was rubber-stamped "Property of the California State Library."

"Dr. Birkensteen was reading about the effects of Sodium Pentothal on brain function," said Jupe.

"Sodium Pentothal is an anesthetic," said Terreano. "It deadens feeling. And makes you lose consciousness."

Jupe picked up a second magazine. It was a copy of the *Journal of the American Medical Association*, and it contained an article on nitrous oxide.

"Another anesthetic," said Brandon. "It's used in dentistry a lot. They call it laughing gas."

There were other magazines and other articles. All were on anesthetics of one type or another.

"Well, of course," said Terreano. "He operated on the chimps from time to time. He needed anesthetics."

"And yesterday an entire town was put to sleep," said Jupe quietly.

Jupe and the two men searched the lab. They found nothing that could possibly be used as an anesthetic. There was no ether, no Sodium Pentothal. There wasn't even any Novocain.

When Jupe left the laboratory at last, his thoughts were on Eleanor. Could she have taken the notes? If so, why? And had she destroyed the pages from the calendar? If so, why? She was too timid to have taken part in a theft.

Or was she?

Questions and
More Questions

By noon Pete Crenshaw had decided he was
wasting his time. Centerdale was larger than
Citrus Grove, but not much different. There
were two supermarkets instead of just one, and
four gas stations instead of two. The Greyhound
bus didn't stop in front of the drugstore. It
stopped at the Centerdale Hotel. There was
nothing suspicious-looking. Besides, Pete didn't
know exactly what he was looking for.

He sighed and wished that he had gone to the
Spicer Foundation with Jupe. No sooner had
this thought crossed his mind when a dusty old

car passed him on the street and turned a corner.

Driving it was Frank DiStefano.

Pete sprinted to the intersection where the young handyman had turned. He saw DiStefano pull into the driveway of a shabby house halfway down a tree-lined street. DiStefano parked in the drive and went into the house carrying a brown-paper parcel.

Pete waited. After a minute or two DiStefano came out again. He got into his car, backed out of the drive, and came toward Pete.

Pete looked away as DiStefano neared the corner. After DiStefano turned and sped off in the direction of Citrus Grove, Pete walked down the street to the house where the handyman had parked. He stood staring at it. He was wondering what his next move should be when a car came down the street and turned into the driveway. It stopped and a plump woman with short gray hair got out.

"Did you want something?" she said to Pete.

"No, ma'am," said Pete. He paused for a second to think of an excuse for loitering there, then he gave a friendly grin. "I was wondering if I could get a lift back to Citrus Grove with Frank DiStefano. I mean, if he should be coming back here. I just saw him drive away."

"Oh, you should have called to him," said the

woman. "I'm afraid he's gone for the day."

She looked concerned. "Don't you have any way to get to Citrus Grove?" she said nervously. "You won't hitchhike, I hope. It's so dangerous!"

"No, ma'am," said Pete. "I can take the bus."

"All right, then." She opened the trunk of the car and started to take out a sack of groceries. Pete hurried to help, and she murmured her thanks and led the way to the side door of the house.

"Are you Mrs. DiStefano?" asked Pete.

"Frank's mother? No indeed. I'm his landlady. He rents a room from me."

Pete put the groceries down on the kitchen table.

"Do you live in Citrus Grove?" said the woman. Without waiting for an answer, she continued. "Were you there yesterday when that spooky thing happened and everyone went to sleep? I'll bet there's something getting into our drinking water. The authorities ought to look into it."

"They did," said Pete. "They analyzed the water at the crime lab. There wasn't anything in it."

The woman shook her head. "It's scary. I could have shot Frank yesterday. Of all days to be sick, he had to pick yesterday and miss all the excitement. Of course, it's a wonder he isn't sick more often, up till all hours playing that stereo. Yesterday all he could do was lie in bed all morning snoring. If he'd gone to Citrus Grove, he could have told me all about it. I suppose he would have noticed a few' things, even if he is so wrapped up in himself that he hardly knows that other people are alive. I would have gone to see the cave myself, but where would I have parked?"

"I don't know," said Pete. He began to back out of the kitchen.

"Should I tell Frank you were here?" asked the woman. "What name should I say? Not that he gets interested enough to pay a lot of attention to names, but you never can tell."

"Pete," said Pete. "He may not remember me."

"I'll tell him anyway," she promised.

Pete escaped and went back to the main street, where he caught the bus to Citrus Grove.

Pete found Jupiter sitting in an old swing in the McAfees' backyard. Jupe listened to the report on Centerdale and sighed.

"So Frank DiStefano really was sick yesterday morning," Jupe said. "I wondered if he might not have had something to do with the kidnapping, but I guess not. He was the only person we know who had no alibi, and now he has one." He shrugged. "So it goes."

Pete stretched out on the grass, and Jupe sat brooding and pulling at his lip in a way that signaled intense concentration. Bob found the two of them there when he returned at four o'clock.

"Well?" said Jupe as Bob came up the drive.

"Birkensteen had an appointment with Dr. Henry Childers the day he died," Bob announced triumphantly. "Childers lives on Harborview Lane. He's an anesthesiologist who practices at St. Brendan's Hospital in Santa Monica. When I asked him whether Dr. Birkensteen had left his briefcase there in May, he jumped as if a wasp had stung him. He'd waited for Birkensteen all that day, and Birkensteen never showed. Of course, he later found out about Birkensteen's death."

"An anesthesiologist?" said Jupe. "Was he a friend of Birkensteen's?"

"No. A mutual friend at UCLA suggested that he and Birkensteen might meet. He didn't know why Birkensteen wanted to see him, and neither did the UCLA friend. Anyway, I thought it was super interesting that he was an anesthesiologist, so I asked him whether there was an anesthetic so powerful that it could put an entire town to sleep in seconds."

"Ah!" said Jupe. "What did he say?"

"He said no. He'd heard about what happened here yesterday, but he still said no."

"Um!" said Jupe.

Just then Eleanor came out on the back porch, nodded to the boys, and headed for the barn. Her uncle followed her outside.

"Ellie, where you goin'?" called Newt.

"Doris Clayton asked me to supper," said Eleanor.

"Well, mind you're home early," warned Newt.

The pickup truck roared and Eleanor backed out of the barn.

Her uncle stood watching her as she drove away.

Jupe came forward from the swing, clearing his throat so that McAfee turned and faced him.

"I was just wondering," Jupe said, "have you heard anything more from the kidnapper?"

"No," said McAfee, disgusted. "And I don't know as I'll tell you when I do." And he stomped inside.

The boys spent part of the evening at the Lazy Daze Café wondering about anesthetics, and part of the evening wandering through town.

Eleanor returned home after midnight. Up in the loft the boys heard her drive the truck into the barn. They also heard Newt McAfee call from the house, demanding to know where she had been until this hour. After she went into the house, the windows were slammed down, and the sounds of raised voices and weeping were muffled.

"Golly!" said Pete. "How old is she, anyway? They treat her like a little girl."

"She's old enough to walk away," Bob said.

Things were quiet at the house at last, and the boys dropped off to sleep. They were up early Monday morning and out before anyone in the house was stirring. After breakfast they called Les Wolf to find out when he was return-ing to Rocky Beach and were happy to learn that he needed to stay in Citrus Grove at least one more day.

The boys were walking back up Main Street when they saw Eleanor drive the truck down the road. She pulled into the gas station near the park and began to put gasoline into the truck.

"She must really have been out joy riding with her girl friend last night," said Bob. "I saw Newt McAfee fill that tank yesterday, and if it's out of gas this morning . . ."

But Bob stopped, for the pump shut off just after the bell rang for the second time. Eleanor removed the hose from the tank, put the cap back on, and took money out of her pocket to pay the attendant.

"Two gallons and a bit more," said Jupe, watching Eleanor drive away. "That would be about forty miles on that truck. She could have driven as far as Centerdale, couldn't she?"

"Maybe that girl friend lives in Centerdale," said Pete. "Or maybe she went to meet someone else. Maybe she's topping off the tank so that her uncle won't wonder where all the gas went."

Jupiter grimaced. "We have no reason to suspect that," he said. "We really don't have a reason to suspect her of anything at all. It's all speculation. Maybe it would be wiser—and more efficient—to simply get everything out in the open and ask her whether she knows anything about the cave man that might be helpful."

"She'll lie," said Bob. "She's lying about the trip to Rocky Beach, isn't she?"

"I think so. But she seems very much alone, and she might be relieved to talk to someone. What have we got to lose?"

"Nothing," said Bob, "only if you want to talk to her, maybe you'd better do it alone. She'll cry, for one thing, and that always makes me feel like a crumb. And we don't want it to look like we're ganging up on her."

"All right," said Jupe.

When the boys reached the McAfee house, they found that Eleanor had already gone up to the foundation, so Jupe left his friends and went up the road after her. He was about to ring the foundation's doorbell when he heard Eleanor shouting.

"What do you mean it's too late?" she cried. "It can't be too late!"

Jupe backed away from the door. The living room window was open, and he turned and looked in.

No one was there. The animal heads on the wall stared blankly into the room.

"I don't care if you've already called him," said Eleanor. "Call him back. Tell him it was all a joke!"

Jupe remembered that there was a telephone on the wall in the hallway outside the laboratories. Evidently Eleanor was using this phone.

"You're a liar!" she snapped. "You didn't do it for me. You don't care what happens to me!"

There was a brief silence. Then Eleanor said, "All right, you'll find out what I'm going to do."

The receiver crashed down.

Jupe stepped away from the window. An instant later the front door was snatched open and Eleanor came out. Her head was up and her lips were set, and she did not glance to the left or the right as she dashed down the steps and out the gate.

Jupe went after her, but he did not call out. He was halfway down the road when he saw her cross the field by the McAfee house and throw open the barn door. Pete and Bob came to the loft window and watched as the pickup truck backed out. Eleanor made a hasty, jolting turn, then sped into the road and was gone, racing through the town.

Pete and Bob came out of the barn as Jupe reached it.

"Where's she off to?" Pete asked.

"I don't know," said Jupe. "She's very angry about something. I think she's finally going to take some action."

"She's not the only one," said Bob. "Newt McAfee came out about ten minutes ago looking all grim and determined, and his wife was yelling after him to not spend any more money. She said they'd wasted enough on that cave man already. He didn't seem to hear her. He went on down into the town."

"The ransom," said Jupe after a moment. "He's going to pay the ransom! Things are breaking at last!"

A Double Surprise

"Come on!" ordered Jupe. "Let's see how Newt handles the ransom payment!" He trotted off toward town.

"How's he going to pay it?" demanded Pete as he caught up with Jupe. "He didn't take the car."

"Then he's making arrangements," said Jupe impatiently. "Come on!"

The boys went down Main Street. They were just passing the little park when they saw McAfee come out of the Lazy Daze Café. Mr. Carlson, the café owner, was with him, and so

were two other men. Jupe recognized one as
the man who ran the drugstore. As the four
headed for the bank on the corner, they were
joined by a man who came hurrying from the
motel.

"Just as I suspected," said Jupe. "All the
merchants in town have a stake in the cave man,
and they're all going to contribute to the ransom."

Jupe sat down on one of the park benches. He
saw through the plate-glass window that the
bank manager came from behind his desk to
meet the men. He looked very serious as he
shook hands with Newt, nodded to the other
men, then ushered the group into a room at the
rear of the bank.

"What do we do now?" wondered Bob.

"We wait," said Jupe. "And we shouldn't
have to wait long."

Five minutes later, as the clock in the church
tower was striking ten, Newt McAfee came out
of the bank. He carried a canvas money sack.
The café owner was with him.

"Aha!" said Jupiter.

McAfee and his companion went to the parking lot next to the café. They got into a Volks-
wagen that was parked there and drove off.

"I have a feeling they won't be gone long,"
said Jupe. He gestured toward the bank across

the street. The two men who had entered the bank with McAfee were coming out now with the bank manager. They stood on the sidewalk for a few minutes, looking anxious and uncertain. Then they went into the Lazy Daze Café and sat in a booth near the counter.

The boys waited as the church clock struck ten fifteen and ten thirty. Then Newt and his companion came driving up the street and parked. When they walked into the café, Newt was not carrying the money sack.

"Do we dare join the party?" said Jupe.

He stood up and started across the street. After hesitating briefly, the other two boys followed him.

Except for the men in the booth, the counterman, and a waitress who was filling sugar bowls, the café was empty when the boys went in. McAfee stared at the boys and then looked away. Jupe and Pete and Bob took a table across the aisle from the men, and Jupe nodded in a friendly fashion.

"Are you waiting for the phone call from the kidnapper?" he said.

McAfee's jaw dropped open, then closed again.

"You paid the ransom, didn't you?" said Jupe.

McAfee floundered out of the booth and grabbed the front of Jupe's shirt. "What do you know?" he demanded. "You . . . you're a part of it! You've been spying on us the whole time!"

Jupe didn't struggle. He simply said, "I am not part of anything."

"Hey, Newt, take it easy," said the café owner.

McAfee scowled, but he let go of Jupe's shirt.

"Crime is a hobby of mine, and of my friends," said Jupe easily. "It's more than a hobby. It's a vocation. However, we don't commit crimes. We try to solve them, and often we succeed."

"Punk kid!" grumbled McAfee. He went back to the booth.

"Do you think the thief will tell you where the bones are?" said Jupe.

McAfee didn't answer, but the café owner spoke up. "We . . . we don't have any way of being sure, do we? We can only hope."

Jupe nodded, and again the minutes ticked by.

"Suppose someone finds that money," said the banker after a while. "Suppose someone stops to eat a picnic lunch in that rest area and . . ."

"Shut up!" snapped Newt. He looked ill, and a faint beading of sweat appeared on his forehead.

Bob leaned on his elbows and wondered

aloud where someone would hide the bones of a cave man. "In the movies," he said, "the villains are always stashing things in the coin lockers in bus stations," he said. "There isn't any bus station here, though. Everybody waits for the bus at the drugstore."

"There's a train station," said Jupiter.

There was a deathly hush in the café. McAfee and the café owner turned to look across the street toward the little train station at the lower end of the park. It looked as it always looked —dusty and crumbling.

"By golly!" said the café owner.

There was a mad scramble as the men erupted from the booth. McAfee was in the lead when they reached the door.

The boys raced after them, and they were only a few yards behind when McAfee thundered up onto the porch of the depot and bent to look through the streaked, grimy window.

"Don't touch anything!" cried Jupe. "There might be fingerprints!"

McAfee backed away from the window and flung himself at the door. The wooden panels began to splinter.

A crowd appeared as if by magic. Shoppers came running from the supermarket and housewives hurried from their homes. James Brandon and Philip Terreano had been driving past in

Brandon's car, and Brandon pulled over to park.
Elwood Hoffer strolled over from the drugstore
and stood on the fringes of the crowd.

McAfee rushed at the door again and again.
At last there was a wrenching sound as the wood
gave way and the door popped open.

The crowd surged into the station.

"Stand back!" yelled McAfee. "Don't touch
nothing!"

Everyone froze.

There was only a single battered trunk in the
place. It stood in the middle of the floor.
Around it were marks in the dust indicating that
someone had dragged it in through the window.

"Is that where they are?" someone asked.

The café owner threw up the lid of the trunk
and said, "Ahh!"

James Brandon shoved through the crowd.
He stared down at the remains in the trunk—a
jumble of fragments hardly recognizable as
bones, and a skull that stared at the ceiling.

Brandon gasped. The color drained from his
face, then flooded back. He spun on McAfee.
"What is this?" he demanded.

McAfee backed away, bewildered.

Philip Terreano put a hand on Brandon's arm.
"Take it easy, Jim," he said.

He addressed McAfee. "There's some . . .
some terrible mixup," he said. "Unless I'm

greatly mistaken, these are the bones of an African hominid that Jim Brandon brought here, and . . ."

"You're putting me on!" shouted McAfee. "This is *my* cave man!"

Brandon controlled himself, but plainly it was an effort. "You'll find the fragments tagged," he said. "I made labels to show the date they were found, and the location."

"Mr. Carlson!" shouted someone from outside. "Mr. McAfee!"

The crowd parted to make way for the counterman from the café. "Some guy just called," he reported. "He says if you want to find your cave man, look in the old trunk here in the station like you"—he gaped at the trunk—"like you already did."

"See?" cried McAfee. "These are the bones that came out of my cave. They've got to be. How else would the kidnapper know where they were? Unless . . . unless it was all a fake!"

McAfee's eyes were wide now with fury. "A fake!" he shouted. "From the beginning! All a fake!"

McAfee leaped at Brandon and tried to get his hands on the scientist's throat. "You planted them bones in my cave!" he shrieked. "You just pretended to find them! You wanted people to think you were some kind of a big deal. You been using me!"

Brandon drew back his fist, and Terreano seized him. "Here, here!" said Terreano. "Easy now!"

A deputy sheriff came into the station. He started toward McAfee and Brandon. In that instant Jupiter looked past McAfee and Brandon and saw Dr. Hoffer hovering on the edge of the crowd. Hoffer was watching Brandon, his dark little eyes bright with interest, and the look on his face was almost one of pleasure.

Jupe Finds
the Answer

"James Brandon is a reputable man," declared Terreano. "He certainly doesn't need publicity, and he would never fake a find!"

"He must have," said McAfee. "How else did the kidnapper know these bones were here?"

Jupiter stepped forward. "The kidnapper put them here," he said quietly.

Brandon glared. "Now listen here, you juvenile . . ."

"Wait!" cried Jupe. "Listen! It's so obvious! There were two sets of fossils, right?"

"Right," said Brandon.

"The night before last, Mr. McAfee hired the man you call John the Gypsy to watch the museum so that nobody would try to get in. John the Gypsy camped near the museum entrance, and during the night he was awakened by a person he described as the cave man. He came to the barn, where we were sleeping, and roused us. He told us the cave man had walked away across the meadow, and that he had shaggy hair and wore an animal skin of some sort.

"Now whatever John the Gypsy saw, it wasn't the prehuman creature whose remains had been in the cave. I believe he saw someone who had disguised himself as a cave man and who had somehow gotten a key to the museum, perhaps from McAfee's kitchen. The thief took the fossils from the floor of the cave and substituted the fossils of the African hominid that had been stored in Dr. Brandon's workroom. The thief then relocked the door and escaped across the meadow with the American fossils."

"Crazy!" said Newt McAfee. "Why would anybody do a nutty thing like that?"

"Someone might want to discredit Dr. Brandon," said Jupe. "Sooner or later the bones in the cave would be examined by experts. The experts would find bones of an African hominid, complete with tags in Mr. Brandon's handwriting—tags identifying the bones as African!"

Terreano shook his head. "But Brandon took pictures of the cave man. Assuming there were two sets of bones, and they were in the cave at different times, there'd be differences. And they'd show in the pictures."

"Would photographs be conclusive?" said Jupiter. "The skull of the American hominid was partly buried. Anyone could claim that Brandon had planted the African bones and then photographed them."

"And that's what he did!" declared McAfee. "He did plant them other bones. And then somebody else swiped them and here they are—and me and my friends are out ten thousand dollars, with nothing to show for it!"

He turned to Brandon. "I'm going to have the law on you!" he threatened, and he stamped away.

Brandon glowered. Then he bent down and began to remove the fossils from the trunk.

"Sorry, Dr. Brandon," said the deputy. "We can't let you take those bones. We'll have to impound the trunk and everything in it. It's evidence."

Brandon grimaced with annoyance, and he, too, stamped out. As the spectators began to drift away the boys went with them. They stood in the sunshine on Main Street, and Pete grinned.

"You solved the case!" he said.

"Not really," said Jupe. "I merely presented one possible explanation. We won't really have the answer to anything until we know who impersonated the wandering cave man, and who put the town to sleep. Also, where are the fossils that Dr. Brandon first found in the cave?"

The boys started up the street toward McAfee's house, but before they had gone half a block, they were hailed by Frank DiStefano. The foundation's handyman had parked his car at the curb, and he stood watching the people still clustered in groups near the train station.

"Hey, what's up?" said DiStefano. "Did I miss something? What are all those people doing?"

"The bones stolen from the cave turned up in a trunk in the station," said Bob.

"Oh, great!" said DiStefano. "What happened? Did they catch the guy who did it? Or did McAfee and his buddies pay the ransom?"

"They paid," said Jupiter, "this morning."

DiStefano nodded. "Good deal," he said. "So now everybody's happy."

"Not quite," said Jupe. "There are some complications."

Jupe had a sudden inspiration. "Have you seen Eleanor Hess?" he said.

DiStefano shook his head. "No. Why?"

"There's something I want to ask her," said Jupe. "I think she may have gone to Centerdale. Are you on your way there?"

"Yeah. Want a lift?"

DiStefano slid behind the wheel of his car and leaned over to open the door on the passenger side. Pete and Bob pushed scuba gear out of the way and climbed into the back seat. Jupe sat next to DiStefano.

The car pulled away from the curb and rolled down the street, past the shops and the train station, and then past the municipal swimming pool, where kids were climbing to the high diving board and then jumping feet first into the water.

"Looks like fun, doesn't it?" said DiStefano. "I wouldn't mind doing that, if only I could swim."

The car sped on, out of the town and down the winding road toward Centerdale.

Jupe looked around at Pete. Pete was holding the scuba mask and frowning. When he looked up, his eyes met Jupe's, and Jupe gave a tiny shake of his head. Pete put the mask down and leaned back in his seat.

Jupe glanced at DiStefano. The handyman was smiling to himself as he drove, and his lips were pursed in a silent whistle.

There was a jumble of small objects on the seat between DiStefano and Jupe—several chewing gum wrappers, a plastic box with the lid missing, an empty soft drink can, and a torn envelope with bright green lettering on the back.

Jupe picked up the torn envelope. It was a list of things DiStefano had to do. "Fuel Pump" was on the list. Also "A & J Auto Suply, ready Tuesday" and "Scienserviss, Wadlee Road."

Jupe put the envelope down. "You don't swim," he said to DiStefano.

"Nope."

"But you have all that scuba gear," Jupe pointed out.

"Oh, that. That's not mine. I'm keeping it for a friend."

"Are you?" said Jupe. His voice was low and intense, and there was something in his tone that caused DiStefano to look over at him, then look away again.

They were well away from town by now, on the open highway with trees edging the road on both sides. DiStefano touched the brake gently with his foot and listened, his head to one side.

"Now what's that?" he said.

"What?" asked Jupe.

"That noise in the engine," said DiStefano. "Don't you hear it?"

He pulled to the shoulder of the road, set the parking brake, and began to get out of the car.

In the back seat Pete frowned. "I didn't hear anything." he said.

"Maybe you don't hear so good," said DiStefano. He was standing beside the car now, bending to look in at the boys, and his smile was mocking.

Jupe sighed. "The scuba gear," he said. "It makes sense now. There was an anesthetic in Birkensteen's laboratory—something that would act very quickly and put an entire town to sleep, and then evaporate and leave no traces. But you didn't want to breathe it or get it on your skin, so you used the scuba gear and the wet suit. John the Gypsy thought he saw a monster with one eye and tusks. What he really saw in that split second before he fell asleep was a diving mask and air hoses."

DiStefano stared at him, his face without expression.

"Eleanor Hess went to see you this morning," said Jupe. "Where is she now?"

Then, too late, Jupe saw that there was a plastic spray bottle in DiStefano's hand. It had probably been tucked in next to the driver's seat. DiStefano was lifting it now, aiming it at Jupe.

Pete gave a cry and started to scramble forward to get out of the back seat.

DiStefano squeezed, and moisture sprayed onto the faces of all three boys.

DiStefano stepped back and slammed the car door. Jupe felt a weakness in his limbs as he began to slide sideways in his seat. The darkness was closing in, thick, shutting out everything. But even as he seemed to fall and fall and fall, Jupe knew an instant of elation.

Now he had the answer!

Escape—
And Then Capture!

Jupe was awake. He knew he was awake. There was the smell of mold, and near him there were sounds of breathing and of something moving.

But it was still dark!

Jupe sat up, feeling earth under hands. Someone whimpered in the blackness.

"Who's that?" said Jupe. He reached out and touched someone. There was a shriek.

"Eleanor?" said Jupe. "Eleanor Hess?"

"Stop it!" cried Eleanor. "Leave me alone!"

Pete groaned somewhere nearby, and Bob mumbled something.

"It's all right," said Jupe. He kept his voice calm. "It's me, Jupiter Jones. Pete, are you okay? Bob?"

"I . . . I'm fine," said Pete. "Where the heck are we?"

"Bob?" Jupe called.

"Okay," Bob said.

"Eleanor, do you know where we are?" Jupe asked.

"An old church," she said. "It's all deserted and falling down. There's a cellar under the floor where they put . . . they put dead bodies!"

She began to cry now—deep, wrenching sobs. "We'll never get out! Nobody ever comes here!"

"Oh, wow!" moaned Pete.

"The crypt," said Jupe, "in the ruined church. But . . . but, Eleanor, there has to be a way out. How did we get in?"

"There's a trap door at the top of the stairs," said Eleanor, "but it's fastened shut. I saw it for a minute when Frank opened it and looked down, but then he put me to sleep again."

"With that spray bottle," said Jupe.

Eleanor sniffled in the dark. She sounded as if she were trying to get control of herself.

"I got so mad at Frank," she said. "I went to see him this morning. I told him I'd call the sheriff if he didn't give back the cave man, and he'd go to jail. He said if he went to jail, I'd go too. But I didn't care!"

"Is that when he zapped you with the spray stuff?" Pete asked.

"Yes. And when I woke up here in the dark, I was so scared. I yelled and yelled, but nobody came and I was afraid to . . . to move, in case there might be a hole, or snakes or something. And after a long while Frank opened the trap door and I saw where I was. I started to go up the stairs, but Frank squirted some more of that formula on me, and I went to sleep again. I guess that's when he put you in here."

"The formula in Frank's spray bottle was developed by Dr. Birkensteen, wasn't it?" said Jupe.

"Yes. He called it 4–23 because he first used it on April twenty-third. He said the chimps were living too fast and dying too soon, and he wanted to stop that from happening. The formula put the chimps to sleep, and that's all it did. Dr. Birkensteen was disappointed, but he thought that doctors might want to use the formula when they performed surgery, because it didn't seem to have any side effects."

"So he went to Rocky Beach to talk with an anesthesiologist," said Jupe, "and he died there

—before he accomplished his mission. We can guess the rest. You told Frank DiStefano about the formula, and one or the other of you hit on the idea of putting the town to sleep and stealing the fossil bones."

Jupe expected another burst of tears, but it didn't come.

"I thought we'd only ask for a little bit of money," said Eleanor. "I only wanted a few hundred so that I could leave here, and I'd be able to pay my way until I had a job. Frank crossed me up. I should have guessed he would. It's my own fault. But the next one who tries shoving me around had better watch it!"

"Hooray for your side," said Pete, "but we'd better find a way out of here, or there might not *be* any next time."

He stood up and took a cautious step in the darkness, and then another. Then he stumbled against something and almost fell.

"The stairs," he said.

"Just a second," said Bob. He felt his way over to Pete, his arms stretched in front of him. Then the two of them went up the stairs slowly, holding on to the brick wall of the crypt. At last they could go no farther, for there was a trap door, as Eleanor had said, and it was firmly fastened.

Pete crouched under the barrier and then tried to straighten his legs and force the door up, but it wouldn't budge.

Bob pounded with his fists, but that was futile.

"There's got to be a way," said Bob.

"There isn't," Eleanor declared. Her voice shook, but she didn't cry again. "We're stuck here, and if Frank doesn't come back to let us out, we aren't going to . . . to . . ."

"Never mind," said Jupe quickly. "He'll come."

"Or he may not have to," Bob announced. "Hey, Pete, do you feel a draft? Coming through this wall?"

Pete didn't answer, but both boys felt with their hands at the bricks that formed the thick wall of the crypt. They were weathered old bricks, and the mortar that secured them had crumbled and fallen away in several places.

"We must be above the level of the ground here," said Bob. "That's fresh air coming in through the cracks in the wall."

He doubled up his fist and struck the wall with the side of his hand. And then, "It moved!" he cried. "It's loose!"

He scrabbled with his fingernails, and more mortar fell away. Then there was a scraping sound as he lifted a brick out of the wall.

"Hot dog!" he cried.

The brick crashed down to the floor of the crypt, and in the darkness Jupe said, "Hey, watch it!"

"Sorry," said Bob. He got a grip on a second brick, and he dug and tugged and scratched and pulled until it came away.

The third brick came more easily, and then a fourth. Beyond the first row of bricks there was a wall of mortar that fell away almost at a touch, and beyond that was another row of bricks.

Pete put a hand out and shoved with all his might, and two bricks fell outward and dropped from sight in the clearing around the old church.

And Eleanor and the boys saw daylight!

After that it was easy. They pulled at the bricks, and they scratched and picked at the mortar, and they shoved and yanked. Soon Bob was able to squirm through the opening. He was dirty and scratched, and his fingers were bloodied.

A minute later the three remaining captives heard scraping noises overhead. Bob was shoving away the heavy beams and rocks with which DiStefano had barricaded the trap door. While he waited, Jupe studied the crypt by the light from the hole they'd made in the outside wall. It was a long, narrow room, not very large.

Along the inner wall, niches that had once held coffins gaped blackly. Jupe shivered at the thought of how close they'd come to needing coffins themselves.

Finally Bob lifted the trap door and the three in the crypt scrambled up the stairs.

Eleanor's face was dirty and her eyes were red and there was a rip in the knee of her slacks, but she looked determined. For the first time since the boys had met her, she seemed sure of what she wanted to do.

"Okay," she said, leading the way out of the ruined church. "Let's go grab Frank before he can get away. If we don't, everybody could be in big trouble. He took the notes from Dr. Birkensteen's journals, and he's got them now. He's got the formula for 4–23!"

"You mean he can go on making stuff to put people to sleep?" said Pete.

"Sure. It isn't hard to do, once you know how. And Frank took chemistry before he dropped out of college."

"Oh, no!" exclaimed Pete.

They jogged through the woods and across the meadow. When they reached the barn, they found the car was there with the keys in the ignition. Thalia McAfee must have just returned from grocery shopping, for there were sacks in the back filled with canned goods and bread and produce.

Eleanor leaped behind the wheel and reached for the keys.

"Hey, wait a second!" yelled Pete. He snatched open the back door and jumped in. Bob climbed in behind him, and Jupe sprinted around the car and got in next to Eleanor.

Thalia McAfee popped out of the back door of the house and shouted as Eleanor gunned the motor and roared backward out of the barn. Eleanor ignored her. She shifted gears, jounced toward the road, and sped toward town.

"Where are we going?" asked Jupe.

For the first time Eleanor faltered. She slackened speed and looked at Jupe in panic.

"I . . . I thought maybe Centerdale," she said.

Jupe looked worried. "Frank is probably running," he said. "He's most likely afraid that we might manage to get out of the crypt, or that we'd be missed and there would be a search."

"But he's got to be in Centerdale!" cried Eleanor. "He wouldn't hurry, would he? He wouldn't think we'd get out so fast! If we don't get him, it will be really terrible. He could make gallons of Dr. Birkensteen's formula. He could put the whole country to sleep."

Eleanor pulled into the parking lot next to the café. "I'll call the sheriff," she declared. "I'll tell them to get out an alert for him."

"Wait a second," said Jupe. He closed his eyes and pictured the list of errands he had seen in Frank DiStefano's car.

"What is it?" said Eleanor. She seized his arm and shook him. "Hey, let's not waste more time, huh?"

"Easy!" Pete warned. "Jupe's trying to remember something."

"Wadlee Road," said Jupe. "Where's Wadlee Road?"

"It's a little industrial section in Centerdale."

"Then that's it!" cried Jupe. "There was a name on that list. Scienserviss. It probably stands for Science Service. It must be the name of some company that sells chemicals. DiStefano's going to buy the things he needs to make more formula."

"Oh!" said Eleanor. Then she was out of the car and groping for change for the pay telephone in the parking lot.

"Here!" Bob stood beside her, holding out some coins.

A dime plunked into the telephone, and Eleanor dialed. She waited perhaps twenty seconds, then said, "This is Eleanor Hess, Newt McAfee's niece. The man who stole the fossil bones from the cave in Citrus Grove is Frank DiStefano. Right now he's probably at Science Service on Wadlee Road in Centerdale, buying chemicals to make more of that formula that puts people to sleep. When your men go to pick him up, they should be careful. He can knock them out if they aren't."

Eleanor hung up, and she and Bob ran back to the car. Eleanor zoomed out of the parking lot and headed for Centerdale.

"I sure hope they were listening good at the sheriff's station," said Eleanor.

"So do I," Jupe agreed.

They were clear of the town now, and Eleanor's foot came down on the accelerator. The woods on either side of the road flashed by. Jupe planted his feet against the floorboards and braced himself as they sped around curves.

No one spoke until they passed the sign announcing that they were entering Centerdale. Then Eleanor stepped on the brake, and the car almost skidded as they slowed to the legal limit.

"We don't want to get stopped now," said Eleanor.

They rolled past the two supermarkets that faced each other across the street, and Eleanor turned right. The boys saw smaller shops and a few houses, and then they were among industrial buildings. Eleanor turned again.

"This is Wadlee Road," she said, "but I don't see any car from the sheriff's department."

Then they spotted a square, windowless building with a sheriff's car near the loading dock. DiStefano's car was next to it. DiStefano was standing beside the sheriff's car with his spray bottle in his hand.

DiStefano whirled, saw them coming, then leaped toward his own car.

Eleanor turned into the driveway of the chemical company. The boys saw that the one officer in the sheriff's car was slumped forward with his head on the steering wheel. They saw DiStefano behind the wheel of his car. His face was distorted and he was shouting something. The grinding of his engine resounded across the lot. He was trying to start his car, and it was stalling and stalling.

It caught at last and jerked into motion. The tires squealed on the pavement as DiStefano sped toward the road.

Eleanor Hess yanked hard on her steering wheel.

There was a jolting crash, and then a clanging, jangling sound as metal parts bounced to the pavement. Eleanor had caught Frank DiStefano's right front side, crushing his fender against the wheel.

DiStefano shouted a curse and scrambled out of his car. He ran toward Eleanor, his spray bottle in hand.

Instantly Pete was out of the back seat, with something hard and dark and round in his hand. He threw it, and it caught DiStefano on the forehead. DiStefano staggered, dropped his spray bottle, and fell, stumbling backward over his own feet.

There were sirens and flashing lights on the road, and a second sheriff's car pulled into the lot. It screeched to a stop just a few feet from DiStefano. Officers got out with guns drawn. They looked down at DiStefano, and then they looked at Eleanor and the boys.

"There were all these groceries in the back," said Pete brightly, "so I beaned him with an eggplant!"

The Million-Dollar Motive

The deputy sheriff sat on the terrace behind the Spicer mansion and looked with open longing at the swimming pool that sparkled in Tuesday morning's sun.

"We have a good case against DiStefano," he said. "His fingerprints are on the trunk we found at the old train station yesterday. Also, his landlady identified the trunk. He swiped it out of her attic."

The officer looked around at the people who had gathered on the terrace. Newt and Thalia McAfee had come in response to a call from

Terreano. Eleanor Hess, who had spent the night with Mrs. Collinwood, was sitting close to the housekeeper. Now and then Mrs. Collinwood reached out and patted her arm in a comforting way.

Jupiter, Pete, and Bob had spent part of the evening with the sheriff's men in Centerdale and then had returned to Citrus Grove with Eleanor. They had seen the McAfees start up the road that morning and had trailed along.

Philip Terreano and James Brandon had come out of their workrooms. Dr. Hoffer, who had been in the pool when the deputy sheriff arrived, had climbed out, wrapped himself in a towel, and joined the circle on the terrace.

"What about my cave man?" said Newt McAfee. "When do I get him back?"

"The bones in that trunk are not your cave man!" cried Brandon. "They are the bones of my African hominid!"

"There *were* two fossil individuals," said Terreano. "There simply had to be two!"

"Then why don't you ask *her*?" Thalia McAfee pointed to Eleanor. "Wouldn't put it past her to have taken those bones and hid them, just to be ornery."

Eleanor's head came up in defiance. "No. I don't know anything more than . . . than what I've already told."

"If you told so much, why aren't you in jail right now?" demanded Thalia. She turned to the deputy sheriff. "You want us to go down and sign a complaint or something? She's the one who helped that DiStefano, ain't she?"

"Miss Hess is free on bail right now," said the officer.

"Bail?" rumbled McAfee. "Who'd put up bail for her? I sure wouldn't."

"I did," said James Brandon.

McAfee gasped. "You did? Why?"

"Because I chose to," said Brandon. "Anyone who has had to live in your house all these years can be forgiven a great deal."

Thalia McAfee quivered with indignation. "Don't you talk like that!" she shrieked. "We ain't the ones who did wrong. She did it! And after we took her in and made a home for her!"

Eleanor sat straighter in her chair. "I only wanted to get back a little of what's really mine! I wanted to leave here and go to work in San Diego or Los Angeles, and maybe get some more schooling and have a . . . a place of my own and some friends. And every time I had any money, you took it away and talked about how much it cost to feed me. I was going to be stuck here forever, and you'd have everything!"

She leaned toward Thalia McAfee, who cringed back in her chair.

"I didn't want much," said Eleanor. "Maybe five hundred or so. Well, now I'm going to get a lot. I'm going to get a lawyer, and he'll see that I get an accounting of my money."

"What money did you ever have?" cried Thalia.

"My father had insurance, didn't he?" said Eleanor.

Thalia pressed her lips together and looked away.

"And there's the house in Hollywood," said Eleanor. "It's really mine, isn't it? What happened to the money from the rent on that house all these years?"

Newt McAfee cleared his throat. "Now, now, Ellie," he said. "We don't have to go running to lawyers about this. If you want to leave here, why, you're old enough to know your own mind. We can set you up in an apartment in San Diego, or maybe Oceanside, and stake you a few hundred to get started. No need to take on so about it."

"A few hundred?" cried Eleanor. "You think you're going to get out of this for a few hundred?"

"A thousand," said Thalia. "No. No, two thousand."

Eleanor glared at her.

"Five thousand?" said Thalia.

"Ten!" said Eleanor.

"All right, Thalia," said Newt. "Ten thousand. And nobody can say we ain't done the right thing."

Eleanor sat back. "I should have done this long ago," she said. "Next time I'll be smarter."

"And braver, Eleanor," said Terreano. "Try courage. It beats scheming every time."

"Now about them bones," said Newt McAfee. "I want . . ."

"I'm sorry," said the deputy sheriff. "We have to hold the trunk and the bones until there is some disposition of DiStefano's case."

"You'll probably want to hold the other fossils too," said Jupiter. "The American ones."

All heads suddenly turned toward him.

"They're in the crypt in the old church, aren't they, Dr. Hoffer?" he said.

Hoffer sat like a man turned to stone.

"You wanted to discredit Dr. Brandon," Jupe went on. "You wanted to be sure of getting the million-dollar Spicer Grant so that you could go on with your own experiments. You went to the museum the night before it was to open. This was a well-planned operation, and I expect you had borrowed the key to the museum from McAfee's kitchen and had it duplicated sometime earlier. You removed the American fossils from the cave and substituted the African bones you had taken from the cabinet in Dr. Brandon's room. Then you brushed the dirt smooth.

"When you left with the bones from the cave, John the Gypsy woke up and saw you. You had prepared for this eventuality. You had wrapped yourself in an animal skin and you were wearing a wig. Poor John thought he was looking at a cave man."

Hoffer sneered. "Totally ridiculous!" he said.

"I didn't begin to suspect you," said Jupe, "until the fossils of the African hominid were discovered in the trunk in the train station. Do you know how delighted you looked when that happened? It was enough to set me to thinking.

"I remembered that there are dozens of animal skins in this house, and that one of Mrs. Collinwood's wigs was missing at the time the cave man was kidnapped, then suddenly turned up again. That pointed to someone from the foundation.

"When Pete and Bob and I went out across the meadow and through the woods to the ruined church, you saw us and it made you a trifle nervous. So you followed us to make sure we didn't discover the bones. You came into the church and sat down on the steps there—right over the trap door that led down to the crypt. You were sitting on it so we wouldn't notice it and open it."

Hoffer smiled tightly. "This is all conjecture," he said. "I assure you, I do not go trotting around at night wrapped in animal skins. If you want to stay out of trouble, you'll stop making these wild accusations."

"Some of it *is* conjecture," Jupe admitted, "but there is some hard evidence. You are a perfectionist, and cave men did not wear shoes, so you didn't wear shoes. You walked across the meadow in your bare feet. You left a footprint, Dr. Hoffer, and I made a plaster cast of that footprint, so I knew that the thief had small feet—and a hammer toe."

All eyes darted down to Hoffer's bare feet. Hoffer started to move them, as if he could hide them under his chair. But he realized that this was futile, and he stood up, the raised toe on his right foot in full view. "I'm going to get dressed," he said, "and then I'm calling my lawyer."

"Hoffer, how could you?" said Terreano. His voice was mild, but his face was sad.

Hoffer did not try to meet his eyes. He went into the house, and the deputy followed him.

Brandon grinned. "I'm going to call my lawyer too," he said. "Maybe I can try to get some kind of an injunction to keep you from snatching those bones away again, McAfee—at least for a while."

Brandon got up and went in through the doors to the living room, humming happily.

"Fat chance he's got!" said McAfee. "Those are *my* bones!"

"Not necessarily, McAfee," said Terreano. "After all, you're not the cave man's next of kin!"

Mr. Sebastian
Is Impressed

A few days after the Three Investigators returned to Rocky Beach, they knocked at the door of a house on Cypress Canyon Drive in Malibu. The house had originally been a restaurant called Charlie's Place. Now, however, it was the property of Hector Sebastian, the screenwriter, who was gradually remodeling it and adding improvements to make it a comfortable, if somewhat unusual, residence.

Mr. Sebastian had once been a private detective. He had turned to writing mysteries while recovering from a leg injury, and he had become famous and successful because of his novels and screenplays. But the boys suspected that he still felt a certain nostalgia for the old days, when he had tracked down criminals and recovered stolen property. No matter how busy he might be now with his writing projects, he always had time to stop and talk with the Three Investigators about their cases.

On this particular afternoon Mr. Sebastian's Vietnamese houseman, Hoang Van Don, opened the door. He grinned when he saw the boys. "Mr. Sebastian waits for super sleuths!" he announced. "While waiting, he plays with new wonder machine. Please to go in and Don will bring refreshments."

The boys went through the entry hall and into a huge, sparsely furnished room that had once been the main dining room of the restaurant. At first they did not see Mr. Sebastian. However, they heard a soft clack-clacking that came from behind a bank of bookcases that partitioned off one end of the room.

"Come and see what I've got!" called Mr. Sebastian.

The Three Investigators obeyed. They found Mr. Sebastian seated at his big desk, tapping the keys of a machine that appeared to be part typewriter and part television set. As he worked, Mr. Sebastian watched words and paragraphs appear on the screen in front of him.

"A word processor!" cried Jupiter.

"Isn't it great!" said Mr. Sebastian. "When I arrived in Hollywood not so long ago, I had an old Royal typewriter that kept coming apart on me. Now I have this amazing computer. It's perfect for my writing. I can compose on it and I can change things without rewriting them from scratch. If I make a mistake I can fix it just by typing over it. And best of all, if I change the name of a character halfway through a story, I just notify the computer. The computer skips through the stored text and changes the name every time it appears!"

"Wow!" said Pete.

"And then, when I finally have everything set up the way I want it, I tell the computer to print it for me. Now watch this."

There was a second machine on the desk next to the one with the keyboard. Mr. Sebastian touched a button on the keyboard, and the second machine came clattering to life. A unit inside the machine zipped back and forth across a sheet of paper, and words appeared on the paper as if by magic.

"The Declaration of Independence?" said Bob.

"Just practicing," said Mr. Sebastian. He switched off the word processor and stood up.

"I understand you boys have been doing great things while I've been computer shopping," he said. "Come outside and enjoy the view from my new terrace and tell me all about it."

He took his walking stick from beside his chair and limped across the room to a sliding glass door. "Don is all excited because you got your pictures in the paper. He's been making great preparations for your visit."

Outside, Mr. Sebastian sat down on a deck chair next to a big glass-topped table. "Don!" he called. "We're ready!"

The Vietnamese came out onto the terrace with a tray. His smile was wider than ever. "Organically grown feast for continued health and vigor!" he announced as he put the tray on the table.

"Sesame seed and wheat germ soya cakes," said Don. "With molasses. To drink, melon flip."

"Melon flip?" echoed Bob.

"Squish melon in food processor," Don explained. "Pour into glasses with ice and also honey to make sweet. Very healthy. Gives much energy quickly."

Don bowed himself off the terrace, and Mr. Sebastian looked apologetically at his young guests.

"What happened?" said Bob. "Don used to

serve all the instant foods that he saw on television."

"He has become addicted to an afternoon TV show that is hosted by a health-food guru," said Mr. Sebastian.

"Oh," said Bob. He took a sip of melon flip and made a face. Then he picked up one of the little cakes from the tray and tried to bite into it.

"Don't eat that!" warned Mr. Sebastian. "You'll break your teeth. Leave it. I'll get rid of this food later, and we'll go out for hamburgers.

"Now, what about the kidnapped cave man?"

Bob had spent two days typing up his notes on the case. He handed them to Mr. Sebastian and then sat back while the writer read through the file on the events in Citrus Grove.

"Terrific!" said Sebastian when he finished reading. "But frightening too. DiStefano almost got away with it, didn't he?"

Jupiter nodded. "In spite of his carelessness, he almost succeeded. Oddly enough, it was his one attempt to be careful that tripped him up. He destroyed the pages in Birkensteen's calendar where Birkensteen had noted his appointment with the anesthesiologist and possibly other events having to do with the anesthetic. When I discovered that the pages were missing,

Eleanor had to pretend she didn't know why. But I was sure she did."

"Poor, foolish Eleanor," said Mr. Sebastian. "Do you think DiStefano would have gone off and left her in that crypt? And left you?"

"Who knows?" said Jupiter. "He probably didn't bother to think about what would happen to us eventually, and I doubt that he cared."

"The guy's mind jumps around like a grasshopper," said Pete. "He just didn't pay attention to what he was doing. Like carrying around that scuba gear when he didn't swim, and not getting rid of that green pen."

"He picked up the ransom money from under the picnic table in a rest area between Citrus Grove and Centerdale," said Bob, "and he tossed it into the trunk of his car and left it there. The shoes he wore when he stole the cave man were under his bed in Centerdale. With the photograph the sheriff has of the footprint in the cave, they became evidence."

"What made you suspect him at the end?" asked Mr. Sebastian. "He did have an alibi for the time the cave man was stolen."

"I think it was the fact that he was never present when anything happened," said Jupe. "He always bobbed up later. He wasn't asleep in the park with the rest of us when the theft took place. The day the bones were found in the trunk, he didn't even walk over to the railroad station to see what was happening. Any normally curious person would have wanted to see for himself.

"Also, he was the only one who seemed to be associated with all the elements of the case. He knew Eleanor Hess, so he could know about Newt McAfee's keys. And from Eleanor, he could know about Birkensteen's chemical that put people to sleep. He knew the routine at the foundation and the plans for the opening of the cave.

"His alibi for the time of the theft did seem airtight until I realized that his landlady hadn't actually seen him—she'd just heard him snoring. It turned out that he had taped an hour and a half of loud snoring and put it on his tape deck. He told his landlady he wasn't well, turned on the tape, and went out the window and over to Citrus Grove. He didn't have to worry about the landlady looking in on him, because she never did. He didn't like to be looked in on.

"He drove to the Citrus Grove reservoir, probably along back roads to avoid being seen. He put the anesthetic into the water, then waited for the sprinklers to go off. He had reset the timer, of course, so that the sprinklers would go off at ten twenty.

"Once the sprinklers went off, he went down to the museum wearing his scuba gear, sprayed John the Gypsy with the chemical, swiped the key to the museum from the McAfees' kitchen, and went ahead with his crime. He put the fossils into a sack and took them to the train station. They were in the trunk in the baggage room before anyone woke up.

"Some of that has to be conjecture because DiStefano won't talk, but we can deduce what happened. We have a witness who saw his car parked by the reservoir, and Eleanor saw him leave the foundation the afternoon before the theft with the scuba gear. The anesthetic was taken from Birkensteen's laboratory, of course.

"Eleanor was shocked and frightened when he asked for ten thousand in ransom, instead of just one or two, but she was afraid to pull out of the plot."

"Poor, foolish girl," said Mr. Sebastian again. "What will happen to her?"

"She'll testify against DiStefano," said Pete, "and she'll probably be on probation for a while, but she won't go to prison. She's ashamed of her part in the scheme, and I guess that figures."

"She's talked freely and in detail," Jupe added. "She admits that she talked about Newt and Thalia McAfee behind their backs, even though she never had the courage to stand up to them. She resented the way they treated her, and she hated never having any money when they were probably getting a good rent for that house in Hollywood. Yet she was afraid to leave and go out on her own.

"The McAfees had really convinced her that they were the only ones who could ever care about her. She told Mrs. Collinwood at one point that Thalia McAfee said she was such a poor hopeless thing that nobody would ever marry her, and after Newt and Thalia were gone, she'd wind up waiting on tables at some greasy spoon and living in a rented room some-place. I don't think Eleanor really believed it, but she wasn't too sure. And she had no educa-tion or training. The McAfees saw to that."

Mr. Sebastian shook his head. "Vicious peo-ple," he said. "They should go to jail, along with DiStefano."

"Wouldn't that be nice?" said Bob. "My mom says not to worry, though. People like that find a way to make themselves miserable."

"But whose idea was it to hold the fossils hostage?" said Mr. Sebastian. "Was it Eleanor's? Did she think it was a way to get even?"

"Eleanor isn't really sure who thought of it first," said Jupiter. "She had told DiStefano about Dr. Birkensteen's formula. After Birkensteen died, the members of the board of the foundation planned to go through his papers and decide what to do with them. When he learned this, DiStefano suggested to Eleanor that it would be a shame to let a terrific thing like the anesthetic get away. He said they could really make money with a thing that would put everybody to sleep and then evaporate without leaving a trace.

"Eleanor says now that she thought he was joking, and she said something like, 'Sure. We could put Uncle Newt to sleep and run off with his cave man and sell him to the nearest museum.' She claims she didn't mean it when she said it, but DiStefano picked up on the idea and said, 'We wouldn't sell the cave man. We'd hold him for ransom.'

"She still thought DiStefano was joking, but the more they talked about it, the more sense it seemed to make. Eleanor knew it would be wrong, and she didn't really like DiStefano a lot. She says he was always trying to get something for nothing. But he kept talking about how she never got an even break from the McAfees, and he laughed about how funny it would be to put the whole town to sleep. Eleanor finally decided it was all right and showed him where to find Birkensteen's formula and also the key to the museum. She did have something coming to her from that Hollywood house. She never thought DiStefano would ask for ten thousand, and she never thought he'd try to leave town with the formula and perhaps use it to commit other crimes elsewhere."

Mr. Sebastian nodded. "There's almost no limit to the criminal possibilities of a formula like that," he said. "He could rob banks, clean out jewelry stores—do almost anything that occurred to him."

"What he *will* do is some hard time," said Bob. "He's been charged with extortion and burglary and kidnapping, to say nothing of resisting arrest. And just for good measure, it's a felony to use an anesthetic on another person so that you can commit a crime, so they've got him for putting the town to sleep. He's a real creep. He thought no one would ever catch him. I don't know why, but he did."

"It's an almost universal failing of criminals," said Mr. Sebastian. "They never think they'll get caught. But what about Hoffer? Where is he?"

"He's gone from the Spicer Foundation—in disgrace," said Jupe. "He probably will never have to do more than pay a fine, but it's known now that he made a vicious attempt to destroy Brandon's reputation. He'll have a hard time keeping his own reputation. And of course he won't get the Spicer Grant. The board of the foundation has decided that no one will get it this year.

"The irony of the whole thing is that Hoffer might have gotten the money if only he'd kept still and let Brandon alone. His work *is* valuable."

"What about the bones?" said Mr. Sebastian.

"Both sets are locked up at the sheriff's station," said Jupe. "They won't be released until DiStefano's and Hoffer's cases are disposed of. Newt McAfee is hopping mad because he can't open his museum until then. Dr. Brandon is going to Sacramento to see the governor about having McAfee's hillside made into a reservation of some kind so that he and Terreano can search for more fossils. He also hopes to have the bones made available to him for study before they go on exhibit.

"Eleanor Hess will move into her house in Hollywood. The tenants there notified McAfee that they wanted to move, so she'll live in the house and turn it into a residence for girls who come to the city and have no place to stay. It will give her some income while she goes to college, and she won't be lonely."

"I approve," said Mr. Sebastian. "And what about that astounding anesthetic?"

"DiStefano had a paper in his pocket when he

was arrested," said Pete. "When the deputies took the handcuffs off him at the jail, just as they were going to book him, he ate the paper. They think it was the formula for the anesthetic. Evidently DiStefano destroyed Birkensteen's laboratory notes. They can't be found anywhere."

"So all's well that ends well," said Mr. Sebastian.

"Except that we'll never know if the anesthetic could have benefited humanity," said Jupe.

"Just one last thing," said Sebastian. "Jupe, how did you guess where Hoffer put the cave man?"

"It was only a guess," Jupe admitted, "but the crypt seemed logical. Hoffer would be afraid to hide the bones anywhere in the foundation, and he would hardly take the time to bury them in the middle of the night when he was barefoot and almost naked.

"The sheriff's men recovered the bones from one of the niches in the wall of the crypt. The niches had been emptied and the bodies removed to the cemetery in Centerdale when the church was abandoned and the property sold."

"I see," said Mr. Sebastian. "All right. I will flush these strange little cakes and this undrinkable melon flip down the drain, and if you like

we can go to Marvin's Marvelous Burgers and
eat ourselves out of shape!"

"Great!" cried Pete.

"But before we go," said Jupiter, "if you
aren't too busy, would you be willing to introduce this case? We'd really appreciate it."

Mr. Sebastian smiled. "It is a bizarre and,
well, a nutty case, and I am greatly impressed
with your sleuthing. I'll be delighted to write an
introduction. In fact, it will be the first thing I
compose on my word processor. Now I'm extra
glad I bought that machine. At the rate you
boys encounter mysteries, I'm really going to
need it!"

THE THREE INVESTIGATORS
MYSTERY SERIES